Milu Savage and the Gargoyle Hunters

Milo Savage and the Gargoyle Hunters

The Secret of the Moonstone

D.S. Quinton

Development Editor: Alexandra Ott

Copy Editor: James Osborne

Cover design: Florian Garbay

Interior formatting: Mark Thomas / Coverness.com

For Eli,
Thanks for all the great ideas and for giving me
the inspiration to write this book.

Hey fellow gargoyle hunters,
If you'd like to listen to some creepy gargoyle music while you read,
ask your parents to scan the link below. It will play a secret music
track I recorded straight from the gargoyle realm.
It's free to listen to and can be played whenever you want. But
beware, strange things live in the realm of the gargoyles. And you
never know what you may encounter.

Good luck!
Milo

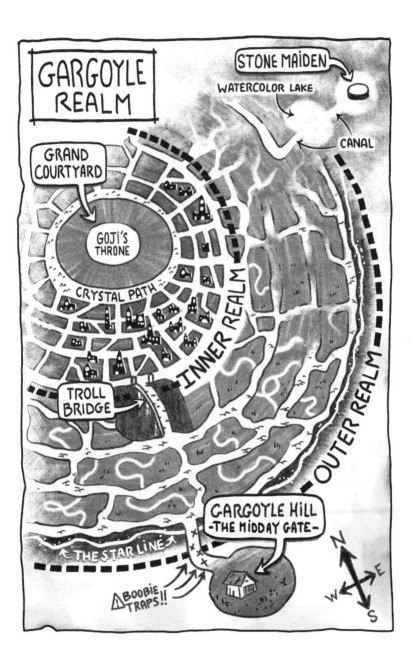

A NOTE ABOUT GARGOYLES

The first thing to know about gargoyles is that they can be *really* cranky. I mean, wouldn't you be cranky if you had to sit on a wall for like a hundred years while birds pooped on your head?

I thought so. It would make me cranky, too.

You'd also be cranky (if you were a gargoyle) because you'd be cold when it snowed, wet when it rained, and hot in the summer. And you could never go to the beach.

What a bummer.

So, yeah, gargoyles are cranky.

The second thing to know about gargoyles is that they are very clever. They should be. After all, what else are they going to do while they sit around all day? Learn how to knit a hat?

No. They sit around all day and think about clever things, like riddles.

You didn't know that?

Yep. And not only are they clever, but they also like to speak in riddles. This means it's difficult to communicate with gargoyles, and even harder to trick one.

And the last thing to know about gargoyles, is that *THEY ARE REAL*. I don't just mean the stone part. Everyone knows they're made of stone. I mean that a gargoyle has a real spirit. They can hear us. They can see us. And sometimes, when the moon is just right, they can escape their stone bodies and walk among us.

What happens when a gargoyle escapes? Well, all sorts of things are possible.

Sometimes good things occur, which means that gargoyles aren't all bad.

But… sometimes bad things happen, too.

And sometimes, very scary things happen. It really depends on the gargoyle. You must remember they've been around for a really long time, and they know a lot of scary stuff.

But one thing you can count on when you're around gargoyles, is that it will ALWAYS be an adventure.

How do I know all this, you ask?

Because my name is Milo Savage, and I'm a Gargoyle Hunter.

MY SUPER REALLY BAD DAY

The gargoyles had been watching me all morning. Their stony eyes saw me approach the large building. Their faces, hard and pale, followed me down the wide corridors. Their mouths, carved into snarls, waited to snap.

I know these things to be true now. But I didn't notice them on my super really bad day. Until it was too late.

It was the last week of sixth grade and my class was on a field trip to a museum. We were all excited about summer break and talked about all the fun stuff we were going to do. Baseball and swimming were the only things on my mind.

It was an OK museum, with a lot of old Egyptian stuff like pottery and masks. The mummies were pretty cool, and I made my classmates laugh when I pretended to be a mummy that had just come to life, looking for brains. I messed up my already unruly brown hair and bumped around with my eyes half closed mumbling, "Brains… brains." I know that's a zombie thing, but I don't speak Egyptian, so that was the best I could do on short notice.

I got a lot of laughs and some squeals. I was just starting my second round of shambling when my teacher, Ms. Halsey called out, "Milo, you can look for brains up here next to me for the rest of the tour."

Ah, man, I thought. *Busted.* And just before I could do my best joke and shamble over to the girls in my class and pretend not to find any brains at all.

What rotten luck. My friend Robbie Martinez could make fart sounds with his armpit all day long, but I get caught on my first zombie shuffle.

So, I did the *Walk of Shame* next to Ms. Halsey while Robbie and my other friends snickered from the back of the line. It wasn't the first time I'd had to do this.

Standing by my teacher I had the feeling that a hundred pairs of eyes were on me. Some of the eyes were from my classmates. But I'd had the feeling all morning that other things had been watching me. Every time I walked past a statue, even the ones perched on the walls outside, I felt like their heads had followed me. You know, sort of like those creepy paintings where the eyes seem to always be watching you.

Pretty soon, we went into a large room with a bunch of statues. All of us kids spread out as Ms. Halsey talked about Greek and Roman history. The statues were huge and stood on giant pedestals of stone.

We saw the Venus de Milo, the statue of a lady with no arms. Then we saw a statue of a lady with wings, but she didn't have a head. A lot of the statues were missing pieces because they were so old, but they were still neat to see. I wondered what the statues would say if they could talk. Were they based on real people? Had the battles been real? What secrets were hidden away in their stone bodies? What stories were planted there when the sculptors created them?

I wondered all these things and began to daydream.

That's when things got weird.

At first, I thought it was one of my friends playing a trick on me. I heard someone whispering in my ear, and when I turned around to catch them, no one was there.

Then suddenly the voices came from the other side, and I spun that direction. Nothing.

We were still in the large room and Ms. Halsey was at the far end talking about something. But her voice sounded strange. You know, like the parents sound in the Charlie Brown cartoons, *Whaa, waa, waa...* like that. And it got softer and softer, until her voice faded out completely. I couldn't hear her at all.

I could see my friends, but they seemed to be fading away as well. They were listening to our teacher, but they looked like they were getting lighter, like I was seeing them through a cloud of fog.

I called out to my teacher, but she couldn't hear me. I called out to my friends. No response. Suddenly I was standing in the middle of a fog bank. The walls of the big room were gone. The ceiling was gone. Even the floor. All I could see was the fog, and the giant stone statues.

And that's when one of the statues looked at me.

It wasn't just the creepy eyes that followed me, like in the paintings. It was worse. The entire head moved.

It was a statue of a fallen warrior. He was crawling on the ground. His left arm still held his shield, and he was trying to raise himself up. He looked like he was dying.

His eyes were pale white, the color of the stone. But when he saw me, his eyes began to glow.

"Miii-lllo," the statue whispered. Its cold voice floated into my head, and the hairs on the back of my neck stood up.

"Hear me, Milo. For my time is short."

The warriors stone arm reached towards me.

I walked closer. My feet moved on their own, as if they were controlled by the warrior. Strange sounds floated through the air, like tinkling chimes. His stone eyes glowed brighter.

"The secret has been found," the stone warrior said. His mouth never moved. I heard his voice in my head. It sounded like it had come from far away.

"What secret?" I asked.

I was scared but couldn't run away. I felt as if I knew this warrior. Like he was a long-lost ancestor.

But that's crazy, I thought. *I don't have any ancient Greek ancestors. Do I?*

His fingers trembled as they reached for me. *"The secret of the—"*

Then he jerked as if something had grabbed him. His stone face grimaced into a terrible snarl. His glowing eyes rolled around in their sockets, looking for the thing that was squeezing him. His mouth opened and closed like he was trying to bite something.

Then I saw it.

A red misty tentacle, like from an octopus, appeared out of the fog. It was a ghost tentacle and it wrapped around the warriors neck and outstretched arm. It was choking him.

"*Mii-llo...*" the warrior croaked. "*The see-cret...*"

His hand jerked back, clawing at the ghost tentacle that was choking his words.

The secret? What secret?

The warrior's glowing eyes began to fade. The tentacle thing was choking the magic life out of him.

I had to do something. So, I grabbed at the red tentacle, trying to rip it away. I was surprised that I could feel it. It wasn't just mist after all. I could feel it pulsing beneath my hands like the slimy arm of a giant octopus.

The red mist stung my hands like it was an electric eel. I pulled at the tentacle with all my strength. I felt it loosen its grip. Then something in the fog hissed at me.

KHHEEEE...

I pulled again and again. Then suddenly, the tentacle twisted the warrior's arm to the point of breaking and disappeared into the mist. I flew backwards and landed on the floor of the museum with a loud *THUD!*

And just like that, the mysterious fog was gone. The warriors' eyes had stopped glowing. My hands weren't stinging. The walls were back. The ceiling was there. And I could hear my classmates whispering as they all stood around me, gawking and pointing.

"Milo!" my teacher said. "What have you done?"

That's when I realized I was sitting on the floor of the museum with the arm of a priceless statue in my lap.

And my day got worse from there.

I GET SENTENCED
TO HARD LABOR

As it turns out, when you break the arm off an ancient statue, you get a lot of attention. The bad kind.

And unfortunately, I was getting used to bad things happening to me. It was sort of becoming a habit.

"You're not a bad kid," my mom would say, after I got into trouble. "But Milo, sometimes…" And that's where she'd usually stop. And there would be a lot of head-shaking and hand-wringing. I always felt bad when mom would wring her hands. It made her look old and worried.

My zombie-shuffle and joking around was fun and all. I liked making the other kids laugh. But I also wanted to do something that would make Mom happy, maybe even proud of me. I didn't want to be a goof-off my entire life. I just didn't know how to stop being one.

But as expected, Ms. Halsey had to tell Principal Skinner. And as expected, the principal had to call my mom. Mom had to leave work early (which was really bad) to come and talk to the museum people. Of course, no one believed my story about the talking statue, or the secret, or the red ghost tentacle. So, after pleading my case, I was told to sit outside in the hall while the grownups discussed my fate.

That's when the museum people came by to give me the evil eye.

Apparently, that's a form of museum punishment. The workers had to first inspect the broken statue, to see if the rumor was true. Then they had to walk by the office of the museum curator (where I was sitting in the hall on a hard plastic chair) and look at me with their scornful eyes. Sometimes they'd squint at me or shake their heads. I imagined what they must be thinking.

What a troubled boy he must be.

Just shameful how these kids are nowadays.

I'd throw him in the broom closet with the spiders!

Yikes! I imagined that last thought coming from the old janitor that had just pushed his squeaky mop bucket past me. Not only had he given me the evil eye, but he'd also made a strange sucking sound with his mouth: *NCCHT*. Like he'd just sucked a piece of meat out of his teeth.

Creepy.

Pretty soon the door opened, and I was asked to come in. Every adult in the room looked like they were at a funeral. Mine.

Mom sat with her head down, wringing her hands. Ms. Halsey had a little frown on her face. Principal Skinner looked at me over the top of his glasses. And the museum curator, Mrs. Gallstone, looked at me like I was a worm on legs.

Man was I in for it.

I'll spare you the lecture about the priceless statue (although its name happens to be *Dying Warrior from the Temple of Aphaia*, if you ever want to see it.) You'll notice that part of his leg is missing (I didn't do that!) But you may also notice that his right arm has a big crack at the top where they glued it back on (yeah, that was me.)

Anyway, my punishment went like this:

Principal Skinner said, "One week of summer school where you will write essays on Greek and Roman history. Hopefully this way you'll learn how valuable history is."

Bummer, I thought. But not too bad, considering there would be a lot of summer left.

Then Mrs. Gallbladder said, "Three days of volunteer work here at the museum where you will clean up after the other school tours finish. This will include scraping gum from the bottom of stair railings, emptying the trash cans, and sweeping and mopping the bathrooms. But under no circumstances are you to go near any statues!"

I didn't even hear the part about the statues.

Bathrooms? I thought. *As in, the girls' bathroom? YUCK! Give me the electric chair! Give me the pokey! The smasher! Anything but that!*

Was this even legal? I wondered. Can you sentence an eleven-year-old kid to this kind of torture?

Apparently, you can.

I could just hear my friends ribbing me during our baseball games about how I'd done three tours of duty in the girls' bathrooms. And how sweet I smelled. I was doomed.

What could possibly be worse than cleaning the girls' bathroom?

Then Mom said, "And baseball will be cancelled this summer.

You're going to stay with your Uncle Horace."

Uh…. Wait, what?

"But, Mom," I started.

"No *buts*, mister!" Now she didn't look so sad. Just really tired, and maybe a little worried.

"We're very lucky the museum has insurance for these sorts of… for accidents. Very lucky. We can't afford—"

"I know, Mom," I said. "I'm sorry. It was an accident. But baseball?"

She only nodded her head.

I put on my best puppy dog face, trying to escape my punishment. You know the one, where your head tilts to the side and your eyes go sad. Alexa Carmichael—a girl in my class—told me that with my shaggy brown hair and brown eyes, I could make the perfect puppy dog face.

Yeah, it didn't work at all.

Mrs. GallBlather said, "Do you feel ill, Mr. Savage? Or are you struggling with a particularly vexing thought?"

Mom just tapped her fingernails on the arm of the chair and stared at me.

Yep, I was doomed.

Great, I thought. I get sentenced to hard labor AND I get exiled for the summer.

The statue already had a broken leg, it couldn't have been *that* priceless. Could it?

Then something occurred to me.

Who's Uncle Horace?

MOM ACTS
REALLY WEIRD

After completing my tour of the girls' bathrooms (I barely survived), and writing three essays on historical events, I prepared myself to be exiled. I tried once more to convince my mom to let me stay home, but she just shook her head, looking at me with sad eyes.

Something was wrong.

It was late afternoon, and we were waiting to take me to the train station. It had started raining and the day felt gloomy. We sat at our small kitchen table. The only time we sat here, besides for meals, was to have serious talks. And this felt serious.

My backpack was on the floor already packed with my clothes. The day had turned gray and rainy. A perfect day to be exiled, I thought.

She also held an old box on her lap that looked like stone.

She had been quiet since my super really bad day and stayed home from work the last two days. I felt like I really was being exiled and she wanted to remember what I looked like before I was gone forever.

My mom and I live in a small house outside of New York City. And if you know anything about this city, you'll know that everything is expensive here, even a small rental house. I've never known my dad and my grandparents are dead, so it's always just been Mom and me. A team.

I'd heard brief stories of other family members, but every time I asked questions, Mom always said, "We'll talk about that later."

Well, now it was 'later.'

"About your Uncle Horace," mom said. "It's been a few years since I've spoken to him."

"I didn't know you had a brother," I said.

"Well, actually he's *my* uncle. My father's brother. So... that would make him your great uncle! How about that?"

She gave me a totally fake smile.

My great uncle? I thought. *How old is this guy, anyway?* But before I could ask, she said, "You met him when you were young. You just don't remember."

I thought, *Must be an interesting guy then if no one ever talked about him. NOT!* But I didn't want to hurt Mom's feelings, so I didn't say anything.

"And yes," Mom said, "in case you're wondering. He *is* an interesting person."

Whoa! That was weird.

Did she just read my mind?

I think she totally read my mind.

"But Mom, all summer?" I asked. "No baseball? The museum will be able to fix the statue's arm."

She waved her hand for me to be quiet. "Going to your uncle's house for the summer isn't punishment, believe it or not."

"My *great* uncle, you mean."

She sighed. "Yes, your great uncle."

"What do you mean, it isn't a punishment? That day in the museum you said—"

"I know what I said. I had to tell you then because I could see you counting the number of days of *hard labor* you'd have to spend on your summer break."

Whoa! There it was again. Some weird mom-mind-reading trick.

She continued. "And I didn't want you getting excited about baseball. When the museum incident happened, I called your uncle before I left work that day."

"You did? Why would you do that?"

"To tell him it was time."

"Uhhh… time for what?" I asked.

During the entire conversation she had been running her hands over the box on her lap. It was a nervous thing, like she wasn't sure if she wanted to open it. Then they stopped. And she set the box on the table.

"I have a present for you," she said.

A GOING AWAY PRESENT

A present? I thought. Awesome! And it wasn't even my birthday. I looked at the box and noticed that it had strange carvings on it. Sort of like scrolly letters, but from another language. The box had gold-looking hinges and a clasp on the front with a little lock.

She reached around the back of her neck and unclasped a small gold chain.

Had she always had that? I wondered. If so, I thought she would have pawned it for rent money or something. We'd scraped by on macaroni and cheese more than once at the end of a month waiting for her paycheck.

Dangling from the end of the chain, spinning in a slow circle, was a gold design. Sort of like two crooked circles connected by two wavy bars. Or maybe it was one crooked circle with three twisty bars.

The weird thing was that I couldn't tell what it was, because it seemed to be changing shape as it spun.

The even weirder thing was that for some reason, I thought I'd seen it before, like from a dream a long, long time ago.

As if the gold thing could also read my thoughts, it spun slower and slower, then stopped.

It was a key!

Whether it had changed into a key, or had always been one, I couldn't tell. But it was definitely a key now.

I watched with amazement as Mom put the key into the lock on the box. I thought it would be too big, but it was a perfect fit. She turned it and the latch flicked up. When it did, a faint light shimmered across the carvings in the stone.

Then the lid opened by itself.

Now, at this point, I thought my normally hard-working, very practical mother would have been off her rocker with excitement. I mean, who has a magic box just laying around the house and doesn't get excited about it? Not to mention a gold thing on a chain that opens the magic box? It was almost as if—

Hey, wait a minute! I thought. *My mom has secrets?*

Now, it's not like I'm a dummy and need to be given all the clues. Actually, I'm really good at solving puzzles, but moms aren't supposed to have secrets! Not from their kids.

Man, this day couldn't get any weirder.

A faint purple light floated out of the box—pulsed actually—like a heartbeat.

Mom looked at me with a funny crooked smile on her face. I recognized that smile. She wore it every time she played a trick on me, or when she was about to win at a card game. It was a mischievous grin. I had the same look when I played tricks on my friends.

She reached into the box and pulled out a rawhide necklace. It was just a thin strip of leather, about the thickness of a piece of yarn. On the end of it hung a small stone wrapped with metal braiding. The stone was the size of a large marble but oblong and mishappen. It was smooth, like the kind you find in a river that has been worn down by water. It was multi-colored with dark blues, grays and purples. It had thin veins of silver running through it, thin as hair. And I thought it must be very old.

"What is it?" I asked, mesmerized by the stone.

She put the necklace over my head. The stone felt warm against my chest. "This is very important. Think of it as a good luck charm. You're of age now and need to learn its secrets. Keep it on and never take it off. I'll know you're safe if you have it on."

"Uhh… safe from what?"

"You're to become an apprentice, Milo. An apprentice gargoyle hunter. We couldn't tell for sure until you reached your eleventh birthday, but the signs are there."

"What signs?"

"The museum incident with the talking statue, for one," Mom said.

"You mean you believe me?"

Mom nodded. "Yes. I'm sorry I couldn't say anything to your teacher or principal. I don't understand *what* you saw, you know, the tentacle thing. But your teacher or friends must never know. No one can. It would be too dangerous."

"Dangerous how?"

"Your uncle will tell you more."

At this point I wondered if mom had mistaken the Chardonnay in the fridge for apple juice.

"I don't understand," I said. "I'm an apprentice gargoyle and I can't tell my friends? Am I going to turn into a rock?"

Mom's eyes glimmered with tears as she smiled. She grabbed my shoulders and said, "No honey, you're not an apprentice gargoyle, and you're not going to turn into a rock. Although, sometimes that head of yours…" And here she rapped her knuckles on my head. "You are going to your uncle's farm to be *apprenticed*. That means he'll train you and teach you."

"Teach me what?"

"Teach you to be a gargoyle hunter."

I scratched my head, trying to understand what Mom was saying. "What does that even mean?"

"It's kind of hard to explain, Milo. But one thing is for sure. It means you're going on an adventure."

I said the first thing that popped into my head. "Mom, were you watching *The Hobbit* last night?"

She smiled again as she wiped her eyes, then as quickly as she'd smiled, a look of alarm came over her face. Her eyes went wide, and she put a finger to her lips for me to be quiet.

Then I heard it.

A strange sound was coming from my upstairs bedroom. A weird clicking sound. The kind of sound that some bugs make, like crickets, only it sounded like words. Somewhere in my bedroom there were talking bugs.

And they sounded big.

A NARROW
ESCAPE

Mom grabbed her purse and keys. I grabbed my backpack and we headed for the back door. Before we could get it open, a red ghost tentacle floated out of the ceiling, hanging above the door.

I couldn't believe what I was seeing. It was the same thing I had seen in the museum. "What is that?" I yelled.

"Oh no! They found us," Mom said. "I don't know how, but they found us!"

Then another tentacle came out of the ceiling, then a third. They waved in the air, quivering. Then, as if they heard me, or maybe they could smell me, the tentacles stopped their random motion and pointed in my direction. They pointed *at* me, like they were looking at me. I could see the underside of the tentacles were covered with suckers, just like on an octopus. Then the suckers began to move on their own.

Each sucker closed like a tiny mouth, then popped open, making a wet popping sound. If you flicked your tongue against the roof of your mouth you'd make a similar sound.

It's how they talked.

"Mom! The stairs!" I yelled.

Long red, ghost tentacles slid down the stairs. They were trying to block the front door now.

"Run, Milo! Run!" Mom yelled.

"Mom! Come on!"

But she was digging through the cabinets, looking for something.

I ran for the front door just as a tentacle reached for me. I tried to jump it, but it swung up at the last minute, snagging my foot. I fell to the floor. *OOF!* And my backpack skidded out in front of me. The little stone on the rawhide necklace popped out of my shirt and clanked against the floor. I sat up, turned, and swung my backpack at the slimy tentacle as hard as I could. That's when the stone began to glow.

The ghost tentacle grabbed at my backpack, trying to rip it away. I think it wanted to clobber me with it. But when the stone began to glow, the suckers on the underside of the tentacle made their weird clicking sounds. Faster and faster they clicked until the sound was almost a shriek. The tentacle was afraid of the stone. Or maybe it was afraid of me wearing it, but something was keeping the tentacle back.

Mom had found what she was looking for in the cabinet. She was throwing something at the other tentacles, working her way to the front door.

It looked like she was throwing salt, but it pulsed with tiny flashes of light whenever it hit them. The slimy things screamed out in pain with each flash. They pulled back briefly, then lunged at Mom from another angle.

A new tentacle appeared out of the ceiling, behind Mom, and grabbed her arm. The jar of salt crystals fell to the floor and crashed. The slimy thing snaked around her arm, then up to her neck. It was trying to choke her!

I ran to her, scooped up a handful of the crystals, and grabbed the tentacle with both hands. I squeezed as hard as I could. I wanted to rip the thing into tiny pieces. It let out a high-pitched scream as the salt burned into its squishy flesh. Although it looked like mist, it could feel pain.

The stone pulsed with blue light. The slimy appendage smoked as the crystals seared its flesh. The suckers chittered in agony. And I felt my hands stinging from the poison on its skin. It was just like the day in the museum.

It finally released Mom and we bolted for the door. I threw the last of the crystals at the tentacles, but they had learned their lesson. They didn't come near us.

We ran outside into the rain and jumped into the car. Mom tore out of the driveway with tires squealing. I looked back as we drove away. Through the mist I thought I saw several other ghost tentacles swarming over our house. It was infested with the slimy things. It looked like long red hairs had grown right out of the roof. They were waving around, sniffing the air, trying to find which way we had escaped.

I never saw that house again.

UGH... MORE RESPONSIBILITY

Instead of taking the train, Mom drove the whole way to a place called Livingston Manor, New York. It's about a three-hour drive north of New York City.

Now, New York City is very big, which makes any other city look small in comparison. But Livingston Manor is so small already, it looks like a speck of dust on the map next to New York.

We drove in silence for a long time. The rain streamed across the car windows, making watery worm trails on the glass. They reminded me of the slimy, slithering tentacles. Finally, I had to ask.

"Mom, what does it mean to be a gargoyle hunter?"

I could see in her face that she'd been thinking about this for a while. She wasn't surprised when I asked.

"Well," she began, "it's difficult to explain. And you'll learn this over the summer. But our lives will be very different from now on."

"Different how?" I asked.

"Well... you may not see your friends for a while."

"What?" I asked. "Why not?"

"But maybe you can make some new friends," she said quickly. "That would be nice, wouldn't it?"

I could tell that she was just trying to make me feel better about a crummy situation.

"And," she continued, "after a while, when you learn more, a lot more, there will be times when you'll have to hunt gargoyles. But you'll also have to protect them, too."

"Protect a gargoyle?" I said. "That's not even real. How do you protect a gargoyle?"

"It is real, you'll see," she said. "You'll have to learn about that. Along with a lot of other things."

I groaned. "Ugh, more school? You remember my last report card, right?"

Mom laughed. "Yes, I do. But it won't be as bad as you think. You have natural talents, Milo. All kids do. Sometimes it just takes a while to figure out what those talents are and how to use them."

"Like a hundred years for me," I said.

"No. Not a hundred years. What are you good at?"

I figured mom was just trying to make me feel better, but I played along anyway. I was good at baseball. But I didn't see how that could help me catch a gargoyle. I was good at swimming, but I'd never heard of a water-gargoyle before, so that was no help. I was good at pretending to be a zombie...

"Yeah, I'm not coming up with much," I said.

She chuckled again. "Your problem is that you don't give yourself enough credit. Just because you have an active imagination, and sometimes the words get mixed up when you read, doesn't mean you can't do great things."

"But what does any of this have to do with gargoyles?" I asked. "I thought they were just chunks of stone?"

"Oh, they're much more than that," she said. "And that will be your task this summer. Your quest."

"My quest?"

"Yes. Your quest this summer will be to learn all you can about gargoyles. To be the best apprentice you can be. Your great uncle will teach you. You never know, you just may have to use your natural abilities to save someone you love one day."

What did that mean? I wondered.

Mom continued. "There are a lot of things in the world that can't be easily explained. And there are a lot of things that seem to have no good purpose, like mosquitoes, or flies. But they're all part of this strange and wonderful world. Gargoyles are no different."

"How do you know this?"

"Because I lived with Uncle Horace as a kid. I heard the tales."

"About gargoyle hunters?"

"Yes."

"But what about the secret?" I asked. "The stone warrior said the secret had been found."

Mom's face had a worried look now. She fiddled with the radio, looking for a new song.

"There are many secrets when it comes to gargoyle hunting," she said. "Closely guarded secrets. Without them, the world would be very different. Your Uncle Horace will teach you those secrets as well. But whatever is taught to you, must remain a secret. Secrets carry a great responsibility."

I laid my head back and closed my eyes. All this talk of learning strange secrets was making me tired. Me being responsible for world-changing secrets? Milo Savage?

I thought someone had made a serious mistake.

THE CREEPY
CATSKILLS

I woke up some time later. Mom said we were close to the town of Livingston Manor. And just outside of that town was where my uncle's farm was.

Livingston Manor is at the base of the Catskill Mountains. There are a lot of creepy stories about the Catskills. But as far as I could tell, the town just looked like any other small little town.

I'd already heard the strange story of Rip Van Winkle, which happened in the Catskills. He was the old man who went hunting in the mountains and fell asleep for a hundred years. When he woke up, everyone he knew was dead and gone. Who knows if it's true or not? But people still claim to hear the gods playing nine-pins on the mountaintops, late at night. The crash of thunder is supposed to be the bowling ball smashing the pins. Some people even claim to be descendants of old Rip, but I don't know if that is true.

Then there are the legends from the Native American Indians who lived in the area. For some reason, they would never camp on certain parts of the mountain. They spoke of strange lights in the forest and bad spirits in the mist.

Spirits in the mist? I'd had enough ghost tentacles for one day, thanks. I didn't think I'd go exploring the Catskill Mountains anytime soon. But then I wondered if there were things *worse* than the tentacles up in the mountains. I had a bad feeling there might be.

I finally had to ask the question. "Mom, what were the red tentacle things we saw today?"

The rain had stopped, and the clouds were breaking up. But beyond the lights of the little town, it was pitch-black outside. Mom said it was because there was a *new moon* tonight, which meant there was no moon at all.

A creepy green glow of light from the dashboard made Mom look like a skeleton-witch. For a second, I imagined she had been possessed by a spirit of the mountain. Finally, she answered me. Her words had a strange, faraway sound to them.

"I don't know what they were, Milo," she said. "Something very ancient, I think. Something you'll have to learn about this summer, I'm sure. Remind me what the stone warrior told you."

"He said, 'The secret has been found,'" I said. "He tried to tell me what the secret was, but then the thing started choking him."

"I see."

"What does it mean?" I asked.

Mom was quiet for a long time. The radio had been tuned to some old rock-and-roll station, and I thought maybe she was listening to it. But then the song began to fade out, and there was nothing but static coming through the speakers.

We had just passed through the town of Livingston Manor and were starting up into the mountains. They were big, but they weren't the giant, pointy kind—like the Rocky Mountains—so I was surprised when the radio stopped working. I fiddled with the knob, looking for another station.

SPLAT!

Something exploded on the windshield of the car, and I let out a yelp.

"Oh! That was scary," Mom said, turning on the windshield wipers. "Well, we're in the country now," she said. "You don't see grasshoppers like this in New Yo—"

SPLAT! SPLAT!

Two more hit the windshield.

"Mom?"

She pulled the lever to spray windshield wiper fluid and set the wipers to high speed. Grasshopper guts smeared across the windshield in three greasy streaks.

"Don't worry," she said. "It's probably just a small swarm. We'll be out of them soon. Besides we're almost there."

SPLAT! SPLAT! SPLAT! SPLAT!

"Mom!"

"Hold on, Milo!"

SPLAT! SPLAT! SPLAT! SPLAT! SPLAT! SPLAT! SPLAT! SPLAT!

Hundreds of grasshoppers hit our car all at once. *This isn't normal*, I thought. *Someone or something doesn't want us to get to Uncle Horace's!*

The windshield was a greasy mess. The wipers smeared guts across the glass. The car's headlights dimmed from all the grasshoppers smashing into them. We could barely see where to drive. The car suddenly fishtailed on the road—like when you drive too fast in the rain—and I heard the tires crunching grasshopper exoskeletons. I looked through the back window. It was really dark now and I could barely see a long line of grasshopper guts squished on the road behind us.

I looked out the passenger-side window. I saw a dark black forest. I imagined it was filled with ghost spirits, werewolves, and all kinds of terrible monsters. It was the Catskills, after all. Then, in the distance, I saw lights.

"Mom, look! Lights!"

The car swerved all over the road now, tires spinning and crunching grasshoppers. It felt like we were driving on ice.

"Hold on tight, Milo! We're almost there. Grab your backpack. If we crash, I want you to jump out and run for the lights."

"What? But what if—?"

"No buts! The swarm is making the road too slick, and I can barely see. If we can't make it up the last hill, jump out and run for the lights. You'll be safe when you get past the lights!"

Then the windshield began to crack.

Now, I'd never considered how many grasshoppers it would take to crack a windshield. They're really light after all, like, they weigh less than one ounce. But there were so many hitting the windshield, it started to crack under their weight.

There was definitely something evil working against us.

"Oh, look out!" Mom shouted.

Just then the car jerked hard to the right, as Mom slammed on the brakes.

The car slid on the greasy blacktop, just missing a gravel driveway that suddenly came into view. We slammed into the ditch with a loud BAM! Steam started coming up from the engine.

"Milo, are you OK?" mom asked. "I couldn't see the driveway until it was too late."

"Yeah, I'm OK. Are you?"

Several more cracks appeared in the windshield. It began to sag beneath the weight of the evil grasshoppers. I was sure now that they were evil. I saw one trying to eat a hole through the glass.

"Yes. But we can't stay here," she said. "We have to make a run for it. Get your backpack."

It had been sitting between my feet and I already had it in my hands.

"Unbuckle your seatbelt," she said, "and when I say so, open the door and run, straight for the lights. I'll be right behind you."

"OK, I'm ready," I said.

Mom looked very calm at that moment. Maybe even a little sad. *That's strange*, I thought. *Why is she suddenly so calm?*

Then she smiled at me.

"One."

I grabbed the handle.

"Two."

I pulled it back.

"Three! Run!"

I threw the door open and bolted out. I scrambled up the gravel driveway as fast as I could. It continued up a hill just like the blacktop road had been ascending the mountain. Grasshoppers flew at my face and jumped in my hair. In a matter of seconds, I was covered with the bugs. And they were biting!

I swatted them away as best I could. I heard their crunchy bodies cracking under my sneakers. I saw a single light up ahead and scrambled towards it. When I got to the top of the hill, I turned to see…

Mom driving away with a swarm of grasshoppers around her car.

"MOM!" I screamed. A grasshopper flew in my mouth when I did. I almost choked and had to spit it out. I crunched it with angry stomp.

Mom had backed the car out of the ditch and was driving backwards down the road, honking. At that moment, I realized why I hadn't been completely swarmed by the bugs when I got out. It was because Mom had drawn their attention by staying in the car and driving away. Yes, they were after me, but they had mostly been attracted to the moving car.

I looked on in terror as I saw a black swarm of grasshoppers swallow the car, as the lights disappeared around a corner. The last thing I heard from the car was the sound of glass breaking. The weight of the bugs had finally been too much.

Then I turned towards the light in the woods and ran.

What happened to Mom? I wondered frantically. *How is she going to get back up the mountain with the bugs everywhere?*

When would I see her again?

Would I see her again?

I stumbled towards the light, fighting off the remaining grasshoppers. I was panting hard as I slapped them from my head and face. I started to feel dizzy, and the light began to go fuzzy. I didn't think I was going to make it.

I don't remember anything else until…

STRANGE
UNCLE HORACE

I woke up with a dog licking my face.

Now I don't mind dog kisses. They're usually accompanied by wagging tails and wiggly butts. Sometimes the slobbering is a bit much.

But dog breath?

BLAH! GROSS! STINKY!

I could do without that.

But I woke up to all of that. And more.

I was laying on the front lawn, with a giant English sheepdog slobbering my face. Long hair tickled my nose, causing me to sneeze. In response, the dog sneezed right back, showering my face with goo.

Oh man… super gross!

I sat up and looked around.

Talk about creepy.

A tall house stretched up and up, looming over me. Lightning from the storm flickered in the distance, casting just enough light for me to see its height. It must have been three stories tall, with peaks and porticos jutting about everywhere. A tall turret (the thing on fancy houses that looks like a tower) stood at the front corner of the house. I imagined that a large family of bats could live up in its eaves.

There must be fifty rooms in there, I thought. *And all stuffed with creepy stuff, I bet. Awesome!*

Old-fashioned gas streetlamps were scattered around the property. One of them lit the gravel driveway I had run up. I could see several others in the distance. Some ran off behind the house and some streetlamps stood in the dark forest. They were shrouded behind thick layers of mist and cast ghostly light into the trees.

Why would someone put streetlamps in the woods? I wondered.

I suddenly had the strange feeling that the lamps were standing guard against something.

Just then, the large hairy dog gave me another slobbery lick, and I heard the front door creak open.

"Gertrude!" said an old man. "Stop eatin' at dat boy. You've had yar suppah! Ayup."

The old man's voice had a distinctive northeastern accent. I'd heard people talk like that before, especially near the coast, where there were a lot of boats. It sounded like he could have been the captain of an old smelly fishing boat from Maine.

I looked up and saw a tall skinny man, silhouetted in the doorway. Uncle Horace, no doubt. No. *GREAT* Uncle Horace, I thought.

He pushed the screen door open and walked onto the covered

porch. He was all arms and legs, with pants too short and sleeves too long. Thick glasses reflected the lamp light from his face and a few strands of hair danced on his otherwise bald head. Suspenders held his pants up over a small belly. Below his pants, worn-out, fuzzy bunny slippers covered his feet.

He banged a cane against one of the porch posts.

CLACK! CLACK!

His voice was high and creaky, like some old men get. It sounded like he didn't have enough wind in his lungs to get the words all the way out.

"Come on now, Gerty, let 'em up."

CLACK! CLACK! Went his cane again. Gertrude, the sheepdog, gave me one final lick, then turned around and bounded for the woods. When she did, her mop of a tail swished my head so hard it knocked me sideways with a thump.

Ow, Gerty, that smarts, I thought.

"Dagnabbit! Wrong way Gerty!" Uncle yelled. "Come back!" CLACK! CLACK!

"Milo? Is that you boy? Watchoo layin' 'round fer?"

Laying around? I thought. *Oh, I'm just laying here waiting to get eaten by a swarm of grasshoppers, then trampled by a big slobbery dog. How was your day, Uncle?*

But I didn't say any of that. I got up brushing grass from my pants and headed for the house. Just as I reached the porch steps, Gertrude (who had turned around) bounded past me and sent me flying again, this time into the overgrown flowerbed that ran in front of the porch.

OOOF!

I flew one way and my backpack flew another. It clobbered a cement garden gnome, burying its ugly face in the weeds.

"Dagnabbit, Gerty. We got ta find yer glasses."

For a brief second, I thought I heard another voice, cursing, but then there was a giant

CRASH!

Gertrude had gone gallumping down the hall. Somewhere in the back of the house something had crashed to the floor.

"Come on, come on," Uncle Horace said impatiently. "You ken see da garden tomorra. Ayup. Da Spickelarks are nestin' and if you value yer hair, you won't tarry." He waved a hand crazily over his head. "Ooo-ooh, dat smarts when dey fly overhead and pluck at it so!"

So, this was my introduction to my Great Uncle Horace. Things got stranger from there.

Walking into the front room was like walking into the Crazy Museum of Useless Things. I counted no less than ten globes, some on tables and some on tall floor stands. There was an antique couch and three chairs.

On the walls hung numerous clocks, all pointing to different times, and at least five hourglasses of varying sizes. The hourglasses were mounted to metal brackets and hung from the walls. This way they could easily be turned over. All of them had running sand.

A Japanese water garden thing made from bamboo went up and down by itself.

Also, on the walls hung a bow and arrow set, three javelins, coils of rope, some steel animal traps, and two pairs of weird looking goggles.

Against one wall stood a bookshelf full of books and maps. And in the center of the room was a large metal sundial that sat on a low coffee table.

Above the sundial, hanging from the ceiling, was the craziest looking chandelier I had ever seen. Metal arms stuck out in all directions. Some of them had regular light bulbs, some had crystals, some dripped candle wax, and one looked like a showerhead with a glass dome on it.

This was just the front room!

"Sit down, sit down," my uncle said. "Let me have a look at'cha."

Until now, things had happened so quickly, I hadn't had a chance to tell him about my mother. But as soon as I sat down, the whole terrible story of the grasshoppers came bursting out. I told him about the crashed car, the smashed windshield and that the last time I saw my mom, she was driving backwards down a mountain road in a swarm of grasshoppers.

Uncle Horace, listening to my story, watched me through his thick coke-bottle glasses and nodded. The fuzzy bunny slippers, with their lopsided ears and dirty faces, nodded up and down, as his feet rocked on the floor. They seemed to be watching me, as well. They looked more like deranged bunnies, if you'd asked me. The black felt eyes looked off in different directions, giving the bunnies a crazy look. I imagined them saying, "Reeaallllyy?? Howww innnteresting… Can I bite your toes now?"

I finished my story, exhausted and scared for my mom. I sank back into the couch and waited for good news.

Uncle Horace clacked his cane on the floor. Standing up, he said, "Ayup, plague of locusts and all dat. How is da ol' bird anyway?"

What? Did he hear anything I said? Old bird? Did he just call Mom, his niece, an old bird?

He headed toward the hallway. "I 'spect she'll turn up in time. Ayup. Now. Off to bed."

CLACK! CLACK!

"Busy day and all dat. Lots of things ta do. Gerty'll show ya around."

And just like that. He was gone.

A ROOM
WITH A VIEW

The idea that a clumsy sheepdog was going to show me around was bonkers. But I was quickly getting the idea that a lot of things were bonkers around here. We were in the Catskills after all.

Boy, was I surprised when Gerty led me straight up the stairs to the second floor, turned down a maze of halls, then went up to the third floor, made two more turns and walked straight into a room with a big fluffy bed.

Gerty must have a great memory for a dog, I thought. Either that, or an incredible nose for food. Because as soon as I entered the room, my mouth began to water from the smell of a delicious soup steaming away on a little table by the window.

The room was dimly lit from just a few burning candles. I felt for a light switch but couldn't find one.

No electricity? I thought. *Is that even legal?*

Gerty looked at me as if to say, "Well, here we are." Then she laid down on a rug at the foot of the bed, and promptly fell asleep. I mean, she literally fell asleep in like two seconds! Amazing! I could hear faint little snores and murmurs floating out from beneath her shaggy coat.

I dropped my backpack on the floor, sat down at the little table by the window, and devoured the delicious soup. It was sort of like chicken noodle, but with a creamy sauce. There was toasted bread, cut into little triangles, butter and a cold glass of milk. As I ate my dinner, I looked out the window at the mist-covered hills of the Catskill Mountains.

I got the sense that my room was on the side of the house that faced away from the road. I could see some of the black forest, with the mysterious streetlamps, still shrouded in mist. I could see part of the gravel driveway I'd run up. It meandered past the house and around the back of an old barn that sat behind the house. Then I could see what looked like a large grassy hill beyond the barn.

Remember, it was the new moon, which meant there was no moonlight at all. The only light came from the old streetlamps, and the occasional flash of lightning. But the streetlamps were so spread out, very little light made its way up to the grassy hill. There was just this subtle glow that seemed to creep along through the mist. And that mist was getting thicker. It looked like rain clouds were floating down and settling onto the side of the hill.

As I stared out the window, trying to see how far back the hill went, I got a sense of movement. I gasped in surprise. Something was out there.

I got up and stood at the window, peering out. I cupped my hands at the sides of my face to block out the light from my room. At first, I thought my imagination was playing tricks on me, but then I saw it. There was definitely something out there.

And it was big.

The more I concentrated, the more I saw. The mist, which swirled around in large clouds, was forming shapes. One after another, the clouds floated out of the sky and settled onto the grassy hill. It was too dark to see them up in the air, but when the clouds got low enough, they came into view and settled into shapes on the ground.

Shapes, I thought. There was more than one.

Then I imagined they began to walk around.

I couldn't believe what I was seeing! Maybe the stories about the gods playing nine-pin and the Indian ghosts really were true. I had to get a closer look.

MONSTERS
IN THE MIST

I ran out of my room, made two turns, went down to the second floor, through the maze of halls, down to the first floor and out the door. It never occurred to me how I was able to find my way through this crazy house. My feet just seemed to know where to go.

Outside, I shut the door quietly, then scrambled down the porch steps only to trip over the cement garden gnome again and go sprawling onto the lawn.

JEESHH! What's that thing doing out here?

Someone had stood it back up, but instead of putting it in the flowerbed, they'd left it in the lawn at the bottom of the steps.

I'll put it back later, I thought, and headed for the grassy field on the hill.

From the front porch, I turned left and crept up the lawn, following the gravel driveway. Around the side of the house, I saw the old barn in the distance, off to the left. Looking up at the side of the house, I saw candlelight flickering in a third-story window.

That was my room! Now I knew where I was, and where the field of mist was.

The field I'd seen from my room was on top of the hill I was looking at. And, it seemed a lot bigger from down here.

My stomach fluttered a warning. It wasn't sure if this was such a good idea after all. But I thought I'd walk just a little closer and see. My feet were already moving.

Past the gravel drive, the grass was taller and wet with mist. I trudged through it leaving dark footprints in the grass. Up and up, I walked. I crossed a dry, rocky creek that ran along the edge of the field I'd seen from my window. On the other side of the creek the mist was very thick. I couldn't see my own hand when I held it in front of my face. But I could hear.

And something was moving in the mist just up ahead.

Quiet as a mouse, I tiptoed through the tall, wet grass, trying to get closer. My heart pounded in my chest. I wasn't sure if I wanted to see what was out here or not, but I couldn't stop myself. My feet just kept walking forward. Sort of like the day in the museum with the stone warrior. Only I didn't realize it then.

SWOOSH! Something flew right over my head! The clouds of mist spun off in swirling eddies.

I ducked and clamped my hand over my mouth, almost yelling out in fright. I remembered Uncle Horace saying something about the Spickelarks pulling out my hair for their nests. I'd never seen (or heard) of that kind of bird, but no bird I knew made that much noise. Unless it was a giant bird. Like a pterodactyl.

I sat down in the grass to make myself as low as possible.

I thought I heard murmurs, whispers sort of, and almost ran away. But I was frozen in my spot. There was something interesting about the murmurs. I couldn't turn away.

Was it the wind making the sounds of voices?

Was there a bubbling stream nearby?

I didn't think so. It sounded like voices, weird, creaky old voices, speaking a different language. At first, they were all jumbled together, talking over each other. I couldn't understand them, but was sure they were words of some kind.

Soon, the words started to fall into a rhythm, a cadence, and they sounded more orderly, more familiar. But I was getting sleepy now. My long day of adventure had worn me out and I felt my eyes getting heavy.

Sitting in the tall wet grass, I laid back to quietly listen to the words. My eyelids drooped and I thought about old Rip Van Winkle falling asleep on these mountains for a hundred years. I wondered again if the tale was true.

A low vibration rippled through the ground and woke me up.

I thought I'd just dozed off and had one of those weird dreams, like you're falling. But instead of falling, I imagined that giant feet had just walked across the hillside.

Their soft touch was just right so as not to thunder about, but their great weight still had energy. It had force. And the earth trembled to its rhythm.

I lay there listening. My eyes were still heavy, but the grass was so comfortable I couldn't open my eyelids.

And just like that, as faint as the wind, I heard a chant:

Tonight! Tonight! We call to the stone,
Bring forth the tides, we're here all alone.
Palaver we must, by starlight of June,
Come out! Come out! Ye old Gargoyle Moon.

At last! At last! Our council is nigh,
Dog star has risen, and Ra is near high.
Palaver we must, by starlight of June,
Come out! Come out! Ye old Gargoyle Moon.

It was a strange chant, almost like a song. I imagined it was sung by old voices in an ancient language. I heard it, and I was sad for the things in the mist. For they must have been very lonely to sing such a song.

Maybe I was still sleeping, I thought, and I sighed.

Suddenly, the hillside went quiet.

I didn't realize how loud my sigh had been, that is, until the things in the mist stopped moving. I sat up.

They had heard me.

I held my breath and didn't move a muscle. The thick fog would hide me, I thought. If I could just stay quiet, perhaps I could—

A giant stone face looked at me through the mist!

"AAHHH!" I screamed.

And the giant stone face screamed right back at me. Only it was more of a growl.

"GGGRRRRRAAAAAAAAHHHHHHHHHH!!!!!"

It was the face of a stone dragon! Fiery green eyes pierced the heavy mist. A large stone mouth stretched into a snarl. A stone tongue snaked out of its mouth, slithering in the night air. And the head rose above me, higher, and higher.

Then it shot towards me, ready to crush me in its giant stone mouth.

BANGALANG
DING DANG

"Gargoyle!" I screamed and bolted from my hiding spot in the mist.

I don't know how I avoided being smashed to smithereens, but I did. I thought I felt its giant mouth whiz right past my head as I ran.

I didn't stop to see if the monster was following me or not. I ran as fast as I could across the field. The mist was as thick as my chicken noodle soup, so I couldn't go very fast. I was afraid I'd crash into a tree or fall off the edge of the creek bank.

I heard great wings flapping in the air behind me. The wind rose like a storm and clouds of mist swirled around me. I felt a great presence swooping down on me, so I ducked and rolled, my hand finding the edge of the dry creek bed. The giant thing pulled up at the last minute before crushing me and turned its monstrous body back towards the hill. It seemed to cry out in frustration.

I felt my way down the creek bank, crossed it, then sprinted across the gravel driveway. I was four steps from the front porch when I tripped over the cement garden gnome (yet again), which was now standing in the yard.

I fell forward, but tucked my shoulder, rolled, and came up in a full sprint.

Who keeps moving that thing? I briefly wondered.

I took the steps of the porch two at a time. I was up both flights of house stairs and in my room before I realized I'd barked my shin on the stupid gnome.

Shutting the door to my room, I leaned against it, waiting for my breath to slow. I listened at the door for several minutes but didn't hear a sound. Gertrude was still sleeping on the rug at the foot of my bed. And the candles still flickered.

I tiptoed to the window and peered out. The heavy clouds of mist looked about the same as they had, only.... Something was different.

If there had been two or three big clouds of mist moving around before I went out, there must have been ten now, maybe even a dozen! Something big had just occurred outside. Whatever the mist-cloud creatures were, something had stirred them up and several of their friends had come to see what it was.

I was too tired to wait around and see what happened next. The clock on my dresser showed that it was 12:27, well after midnight. So, I blew out the candles, flopped down on top of my bed and fell asleep.

*

I dreamed of floating around on a fluffy cloud of mist. I dreamed of Mom, and my friends at school. I dreamed of baseball and homeruns and eating a giant snow cone after the game.

Then I dreamed of an earthquake.

BANG! BANG! BANG!

That's a weird earthquake, I thought in my dream. It sounds just like someone banging on my front door. But I'm floating on a fluffy cloud of mist, so how can I have a front—?

BANG! BANG! BANG!

My room shook this time. It was no dream.

I bolted out of bed and out into the hall before I realized we weren't having an earthquake at all. Someone *was* banging on the door.

I went downstairs as quickly and quietly as I could. I was afraid the banging had already woken my uncle. I thought I could still avoid some nasty punishment in the morning if I could get the banger to go away.

I got to the front door and peered out the top glass by jumping up and down and stretching to see outside.

Hmm… no one there.

I opened the door slowly and peeked out, ready to slam it shut if it were another gargoyle.

Still nothing.

I looked out into the yard (from the safety of the house) but saw only dark shadows. I began to wonder if my sleep-heavy head hadn't played another trick on me. So, I closed the door and turned to go back upstairs.

BANG! BANG! BANG! BANGALANG! DING! DANG!

WHOA! What kind of knock was that? I thought.

How could someone make a knock sound like anything other than… well… a *BANG* knock? Who ever heard of a *BANGALANG! DING! DANG!* knock?

Wee-eird.

I crept back and listened at the front door, then opened it again. I looked out the screen door, across the front porch and past the yard. The same old mist hung around the same old black trees.

I stretched my eyes to the left and tried to look up the hill. The swirling clouds were all still. The night was very quiet. Too quiet.

I opened the screen door and stepped onto the porch. And that's when I saw it.

The cement garden gnome was standing on the porch!

And it was glaring at me.

I PALAVER WITH A
GARDEN GNOME

I looked around, trying to see who was playing a trick on me. I mean, garden gnomes can't walk. They don't even have real legs. Besides, the steps are too tall for them.

"Aarrr!" the garden gnome said. "Ya kick me over again, and I be bitin' yer ankles off, I will!"

The gnome sounded just like a pirate! A very small pirate, in height, I mean, but a pirate, nonetheless.

I didn't know what to say. I'd never heard of a talking gnome before. Especially one that sounded like it should be sailing with Captain Blackbeard. *I must be dreaming*, I thought. *Maybe I'm still in the field and—*

"Well, don't jus' stand there wit' yer gob hangin' open!" the gnome said. "What are ya, a Spickelark hole?"

I clamped my mouth shut.

The gnome tilted its head sideways and looked me up and down with one eye. Sort of like a bird does.

Finally, it said, "Come on, come on. Down in the yard where's I can see ya. I got a crick in my neck, don't ya know!"

I stepped carefully around the gnome—I didn't want to get my ankles bitten off—then down the wooden steps. In the yard, I turned around and saw that the gnome had moved (somehow) to the top of the first step. Now we were nearly the same height.

It crossed its arms over its large belly and stared at me.

My mouth dropped open again.

"How... how did you do that?" I asked.

The gnome looked around, like I must have been speaking to someone else. When it saw no one, it said, "Aarrr, you dim, boy?"

"Uuhhh...," I said. "No."

"Well, ya sound dim! Been drinkin' the grog, have ya?" Here its head nodded over its shoulder, as if to imply my Uncle Horace had grog in the house.

"No!" I said.

"Hhmmm... *must* be dim then. 'Cause hims got perty good grog, he does! Hee! Hee! Heeee!!"

And just like that, the gnome threw his arms up in laughter and toppled over backwards. There he was, laying on his back. But just as quickly as he fell over laughing, he began kicking his legs and flailing his arms, trying to get back up. He kicked and rolled and made awful sounds of grunting and groaning. It was a pitiful sight.

"Aarrr, dagblasted knee!" he cried. "Never been the same since the dance ah '33."

Then, with one loud grunt, he rolled himself onto his stomach and popped up like a spring—*boingg*— spinning around to face me.

His arms worked quite well, I mean... for a cement garden gnome and all. And his legs seemed to be getting better.

"Now," said the gnome, "enough of the pleasantries. We got some palaverin' ta do, you and me."

"I'm sorry," I said. "Some what?"

"Palaverin'! You know, havin' us an important discussion."

Of course, I thought. *What could be more important than talking with a cement garden gnome while giant monsters lurk in the mist?*

"I'm Grimlo," the garden gnome said. "Pleased to make yer quaintness."

I was pretty sure he'd meant to say, 'Pleased to make your acquaintance,' but thought it'd be rude to correct him. Besides, when he'd introduced himself, he'd given a slight bow of respect. So, I returned the courtesy.

"My name is Milo," I said. "Pleased to make your—"

"Yeah, yeah. I know who ya are!" Grimlo said, gruffly. "Enough pollywaggin'! We ain't courtin'! And we got some serious palaverin' ta do. So, take a seat."

I sat down in the wet grass. Then I asked, "How do you know my name?" The thought of asking how it was able to talk had already come and gone in my brain. After all, I *was* talking to it, wasn't I?

Grimlo, still standing on the porch, hopped down the first two steps. Each hop was accompanied by a loud THUD! THUD!

He must have been much heavier than he looked to make such a racket. But then I remembered the loud banging I'd heard on the front door, and in a strange way, it started to make sense.

Grimlo pulled a stone pipe out of his jacket and began to smoke.

To my surprise, it was already lit. "Yer Uncle Horace's told us all about ya. Fer years that's all we ever heard: 'Milo this and Milo that.' Blah, blah and fair thee well."

I wondered who he meant when he said *we* but didn't want to interrupt him.

Great clouds of smoke rose up around Grimlo's head. He plopped down on the step and leaned back like he was on his own front porch. "Now, what in the blue-blazin-moonbeams did you think yer doin' by goin' into that field?"

"Well..." I said, feeling kind of silly now. "I thought I saw something from my window and... and... my feet just led me there."

His voice went high and squeaky. "Oyy! Yer feet just led ya there? Like a poppycock I am, floatin' around willy-nilly..." He flapped his stone arms like he was a fat bird. Then his voice got loud and gruff again. "Bahh! You ain't got control of yer own feet?"

Just then, a long slender cat jumped out of the mist and onto the railing. It spoke in a soft, hissing voice as it walked along the rail. "*Wellll*... let's not judge the boy *toooo* harshly, Grimlo. Perhaps the legend *iiisss* true."

The cat was the color of the mist, silvery-gray, and its bright blue eyes shown like gemstones. At times, when the body disappeared into the mist, all I could see were the eyes floating towards me above a small gray nose. At the end of its silvery tail was a black tip, which swayed hypnotically in the air.

"Ay, Flick," Grimlo said. "Want a smoke?" Grimlo pulled a second pipe from his coat.

Flick the cat shook its head slowly. It stretched out lazily, then laid down on the rail, near the steps. One paw draped off the edge of the rail as it licked the other. The entire time its black-tipped tail swished slowly back and forth.

Whoa! A talking cat? I thought. *What kind of place is this?*

"Does everything talk around here?" I asked.

Grimlo and Flick looked at each other with concern. Then Grimlo nodded his head at me as he whispered to Flick, "*Might be a wee bit dim...*"

"Purrr-hapsss," Flick said.

"I'm not dim!" I said. "Sometimes I just get distracted. But I've had kind of a bad week you know, considering mom and I had to fight off the ghost-tentacle things, escape into these creepy mountains, then she disappears in a swarm of grasshoppers, not to mention nearly getting squashed by a gargoyle... and on top of all that, I had to CLEAN. THE. GIRLS. BATHROOM!"

I crossed my arms and stared at them both, daring them to call me dim again.

Flick nodded and with a shrug of his shoulders said, "Imm-presssiiivve."

"Aarrr-right," Grimlo said, "enough belly-achin'. We still got to address the breach of protocol. Milo, you goin' off into that there field was not exactly part of the plan. You ain't havin' taken the secret oath and all. Now we—"

"What plan?" I asked. "What secret oath? How about someone tell me what the plan and oath are, especially since they seem to involve me!"

"What?" Grimlo said. "You mean yer mom or uncle ain't told ya?"

"Told me what? That I'm to be an apprentice for the summer? Yeah, but I'm still not sure what that means."

Grimlo slapped his stony hand against his forehead. It made a loud CRACK! that echoed into the mist. "Oy... It's gonna' be a long summer."

I MEET A NINJA

I woke up the next morning in my room on the third floor. After my palaver with Grimlo the night before, I'd gone straight to bed. I was so tired I didn't remember laying down. But when I woke up, the sun was already flooding through my window, so I knew I'd slept late.

The clock showed that it was 10:19.

Oh man! I did sleep late!

A steaming bowl of oatmeal with sugar and cinnamon was on the little table by the window. I ate it as fast as I could, gulped down the milk, then ran down the stairs to find my uncle. I had about a million questions to ask him. Most importantly, whether he'd heard from my mom yet.

The house was completely quiet, so I thought he must be outside. When I went past the front room (with all the crazy stuff in it), I noticed the sand moving in the hourglasses. Someone must have turned them over, I thought. Surely, they weren't still running from yesterday.

I walked out onto the front porch and the first thing I noticed was the smell.

It smelled awesome here! Nothing like New York. In the city all you could smell was car exhaust and trash trucks. And if you stood next to a manhole cover, you'd get a big wiff of something like dirty mop water that had been simmering for like a hundred years. Gross!

But out here, the air smelled like grass and flowers and fun things.

And in the daylight the place didn't look all that creepy. The grass was green, although maybe a bit long. The dark forest was just a bunch of neat old trees, good for exploring. Even the sky looked happy.

Then I remembered the mist-shrouded hill where I was nearly pulverized.

I walked down the porch steps and looked left, up the hill. Weird. It was just a plain old field. It didn't look scary at all. There was no mist, no giant clouds, and more importantly, no monsters.

Did I dream all that stuff? I wondered, again.

I looked around for Grimlo. Surely, he was real. But he wasn't in the flowerbed where I'd left him.

Strange.

"Hello?" I said. "Uncle Horace. Are you out here?"

No response.

"Grimlo?"

Nothing.

I walked past the side of the house. The door to the barn was standing open. He must be in there, I thought.

I walked up the gravel driveway to the barn. It was the big red kind with a tin roof. Only most of the paint had worn off and the tin was covered with rust. It looked sturdy enough, but I wondered how long it had been there.

As I approached the door, I saw shadows moving inside. I went in, quietly, not knowing who (or what) was in there. For several seconds I could only see black until my eyes began to adjust. Then I heard something really weird.

"Hi-YAH!

"Ho!

"Ha!

"Kee-YAH!"

It was a girl. And she was practicing karate moves!

Standing in the middle of the barn was a tall, skinny girl. She looked about my age, maybe twelve. She had short dark hair (or it was tucked up under her backwards-facing ball cap), old jeans and a t-shirt. I could see smudges of dirt on her face and clothes.

I crept a little further inside. I'd never seen a girl do karate moves before. Her long arms and legs were like knives slicing through the air. She was pretty good. More than pretty good. She was like a ninja.

She practiced her kicks and punches, over and over. Some of the moves were a crazy combination of arms and legs. I felt sorry for anyone who picked on her.

I wanted a better view. So, I took a few more steps inside, but tripped over an old bucket, hidden in the shadows. It clattered across the dirt floor.

I was still looking down at the bucket I'd kicked, when I heard a loud *THWAP!* hit the pole right above my head.

"Hold it kid!" she said. "Or the next one parts your hair."

She'd thrown a rock at me!

I held my hands up in a sign of peace. She stood there with her right hand on her hip. Her left hand casually tossing a small rock in the air. Each time it came down, she caught it without even looking.

"What are you doing, creeping around?" she said.

"Me? I wasn't creeping."

"Oh, no? You just always stand quietly in the shadows watching people?"

Well, since she put it that way. Maybe I was creeping, just a little.

"I was just looking for my uncle," I said. "I saw the door was open and thought he was out here. I'm Milo."

She stopped tossing the rock and slipped it into her pocket. I thought that was a good sign.

"I work for your uncle during the summers. I'm Kat. That's Kat with a 'K.' Kat Black. And don't forget it."

How could I forget that? She was the toughest girl I'd ever met. She was so tough she might even be thirteen, I thought. My friend Robbie told me that his older brother told him that girls get really weird around the age of thirteen. If this is what he meant, I thought I'd just steer clear of them for a while.

"You do work for my uncle? Like, a real job?" I asked.

"Yeah, like a real job," Kat said. "I live in town. Your uncle pays me to help with the yard and to bring Mazy apples."

"Mazy?"

"Yeah, Mazy, the horse."

"My uncle has a horse?"

"Say kid, do you—"

"Milo," I reminded her.

"Yeah, OK. Say, Milo, do you know *anything* about your uncle?"

"Well, no, actually. And he's not really my uncle. He's my mom's uncle."

"And she's here?"

"Uuhhh… no," I said. "That's kind of a long story."

"Uh huh."

"Hey, what were those cool moves you were doing?"

"Don't tell anyone about that," Kat said, pointing her finger at me. "It's none of your beeswax. You do and you get clobbered. Understand?"

"Ok, ok," I said. "Jeesh, I was just asking. I thought they were pretty cool though."

Kat looked at me like she thought I might be fooling with her. Her foot tapped up and down in the dirt.

Then I said, "Which team?" and pointed at her hat.

She touched her hat, like she'd forgotten she was wearing it. "Oh, the Larks."

"Larks?" I said. "I play baseball, but I've never heard of them."

"The Livingston Larks. You know, the town is named Livingston Manor. It's the school baseball team. I pitch for the Junior Larks, but I'm going to try out for the regular Larks when I'm old enough."

"A girl baseball pitcher?" I said.

"Yeah, a girl baseball pitcher! What of it? You want to get clobbered or something?"

"Uuhhh… no. I just… I mean… I've never met a girl who played baseball before."

"Well, now you have."

"Are you any good?" I asked.

"Of course, I am! I can strike out any boy I pitch against. I could strike you out."

I started to dispute this but decided to keep my mouth shut. Kat's eyebrow had raised up in an arch as if to say, *I dare you. I double dare you.*

"Well, maybe we can throw the ball around sometime," I said instead. "But, I'd have to borrow a glove. I… forgot to pack mine."

Kat's eyebrow came back into place. But that old suspicious look crept back onto her face.

I thought that a lot of people must have tried to trick her in the past. The suspicious look came easily to her.

Finally, she said, "Yeah, I guess we could throw the ball around sometime. I have a lefty or righty glove you could borrow."

"Wow, thanks," I said. And my hands did a quick little happy dance. That happens sometimes when I get excited. It's like the happy energy swells up in my arms then comes out the ends of my fingers all at once. My fingers scrunch up and my hands shake for a second or two, but then they go back to normal. A few kids at school tease me about it, but I've learned to ignore them. Mom said that all kids have quirks, which is what makes each one special. But then again, all parents probably say that.

"Well, I have to go find my uncle," I said.

She grabbed a rake that was leaning against the wall.

"And I've got work to do," she said. "See you around, Milo."

I left the barn thinking, *Well, at least she didn't call me 'kid.'*

A MYSTERIOUS
NOTE

I went back into the house calling for Uncle Horace. He was probably in one of the many rooms, I thought. Besides, I wanted to use the phone and call our house to see if my mom had gotten back.

I looked in the hall but there was no phone. Not even the old-fashioned kind that you see in old movies. The hall led to the back of the house where the kitchen was. Out the back door I could see the barn, where I'd met Kat. No phone here either.

"Uncle Horace," I called, "are you back here?"

No answer.

Off one side of the kitchen was another hallway, which led deeper into the house. More rooms of furniture. No phone. No uncle.

I finally came to a room that looked like a den. A large wooden desk covered with papers sat near the back wall. A fireplace was behind it and to my surprise, had a fire burning in it.

Uncle Horace must be here! And there's probably a phone in his den, I thought. After all, Mom had said that she'd called him the day

I… well, on my super really bad day. So where was he?

"Uncle Horace, are you in here?" I said again.

All I heard was the crackling of the fireplace.

I walked over and looked behind his desk. Still no uncle. Now I was getting a little worried.

A hand drawn map lay on top of the desk. It showed roads that seemed to go around in circles, one inside the other. But the map was incomplete. Only parts of the roads were shown. Cryptic notes were written around the edges.

Snaggler lines here.

Watch out for false stones.

Crushers.

Then the strangest one of all.

Place Spirit Harness here.

I didn't understand what these things were. It was as if my uncle was talking about a make-believe land. Then, I saw it. Partially hidden by the map was a piece of paper. And my name was on the top of it!

I picked up the paper. Written in the same shaky handwriting that was on the map, were these words:

Milo's Training Schedule
- ✓ *Intro to Gargoyle Bylaws*
- ✓ *How to avoid offending a gargoyle*
- ✓ *The Cycles of the Moon*
- ✓ *How to avoid falling into space*
- ✓ *The Well House*

✓   *How to avoid being squashed to smithereens*

✓   *The Secret of the*

And it stopped! Just like that the note stopped. My uncle hadn't finished the last sentence.

THE SECRET OF WHAT?! I screamed to myself.

Oh man, this was frustrating. I felt like I was on the verge of discovering something big. But I needed more answers.

Heck, that was the story of my life. Every test I took in school, I could have used some more answers. But this time I was actually interested in figuring out what was happening here. Something seemed to be waking up inside of me.

I decided I'd solve this mystery one way or another.

I MEET A CYBORG
AND A SCIENTIST

I made one pass through the house, but I was the only one here. So I decided to explore the farm more thoroughly.

Outside, I walked across the lawn, then followed the gravel driveway past the side of the house. Beyond that was the barn, but I didn't see Kat.

The driveway turned into an old road that ran along the left side of the hill where I had nearly been squooshed the night before. There were more fields back there and a few broken-down tractors with weeds growing around them. The old road had nearly disappeared, being covered over by grass. It had become two tire tracks that wandered off through the field, heading towards a distant stand of trees.

I wondered how big my uncle's farm was. There was a lot of old equipment laying around and I thought there would be lots of good exploring to do here.

I walked a little way down the road when suddenly I heard voices coming out of the trees. I stopped and thought maybe that's where the gargoyles had gone to sleep. I went up the hill to my right and hid behind a pile of junk farm equipment, watching to see what came out of the woods.

A few minutes later two kids emerged from the shadows. They followed the tire tracks through the overgrown field and headed straight toward me. As they got closer, I thought the day couldn't get any stranger. One kid was an African-American boy wearing something like space goggles on his face. It looked like a scuba diver's mask with wires sticking out the top of it. Thick plastic straps wrapped around his head. Two metal antennas stuck up over his ears and flopped back and forth as he walked. Wires ran from his goggles into a lumpy backpack he wore. He held a game controller in his hands and would stop occasionally, push some buttons on his game pad, adjust his goggles on his head, then say something to the other kid. He was short with baggy gym shorts, sneakers and a rumply tee-shirt that stretched across his belly. He looked like a cyborg who loved donuts.

The other kid was a girl, about the same height as the space kid, but thinner. She wore hiking boots with tan shorts, a light blue short-sleeved shirt with a brown explorer's vest over it (the kind with lots of pockets), and a floppy hat with a drawstring. She had a book in one hand and a magnifying glass in the other. She looked like a scientist ready to explore the Amazon rain forest. I could hear them talking as they approached.

"You shouldn't let those bullies push you around," Explorer-Girl said. "Just tell a teacher."

"I, I don't know about that," Cyborg-Boy replied. "I'd rather just avoid them. There's less chance of getting clobbered that way." He stopped to fiddle with his goggles, then started walking again. "Besides, as soon as I can get this new software update configured, my face-recognition goggles will spot them a mile away. I'll always be where they're not. Problem solved."

Explorer-Girl shook her head. "But that's not fair. There are rules against bullying for a reason. You really should say something."

I stayed in my hiding spot until they were right below me on the road.

"Hey, you guys," I said.

Startled, they both looked up. The girl held up her magnifying glass like she was inspecting a bug. The boy with the space goggles looked up, and I could see his eyes magnified through the lenses. Two giant eyeballs blinked at me.

"Hey, yourself," the boy said. "What are you doing up there?"

"Just exploring," I said. "What are you doing down there?"

The boy pushed the goggles up on top of his head and said, "I'm testing the upgrades I made to my enhanced-reality glasses. They're hooked into my computer," he thumbed at his backpack, "and give me information about what I'm seeing."

Whoa! He really is a cyborg, I thought.

"And I'm looking for new species of life," the girl said. She lowered her magnifying glass. "We're part of the science club at school. What's your name?"

I came out from behind the machinery and joined them on the path. "I'm Milo," I said, "and this is my uncle's farm. I just got here yesterday and was looking around."

The boy said, "I'm Sammy Ballerini. Formerly of the New Jersey Ballerinis, but we moved out here three years ago. The old neighborhood was going kaplooey."

I knew what he meant right away. New Jersey was a rough city.

"And I'm Suzy Chang," the girl said. "We've always lived here. My parents are teachers at the high school."

Bumm-mer! I thought. I bet she can't get away with anything! But that did explain the adventurer clothes she wore.

"I'm Milo Savage. What can you see with those things?" I pointed at Sammy's goggles.

"Lots of stuff," Sammy said. "The software running my goggles can identify an object, like a tree, then tell me what it is. It says 'tree.'"

I scratched my head. I wasn't sure why someone would need special glasses to tell them what a tree was, but I had to remember the Catskills were a weird place.

"That's just a simple example," Sammy said. "Stand back and let me test it on that pile of junk."

He slid the goggles over his eyes, hit a few buttons on his controller, then stepped towards the pile of junk.

"Tractor," he said. "It sees a tractor."

I looked at the junk pile. I'd seen pictures of tractors before, but with all the weeds growing up around the pile, I wasn't sure what it was. "Hey, you're right," I said. "It is, or... used to be, a tractor."

Sammy walked closer. "Equipment." He pointed to the lump of metal that was behind the 'tractor.' "Axe." He pointed to a different spot. "Hey check it out. A real axe."

Suzy and I walked up to the lump of rusted metal. Lying on the edge of the old trailer (his goggles called it 'equipment') was a rusted axe head. The wooden handle was mostly rotted, and we had to hit the axe several times to get it unstuck, but it was an axe.

"Cool," I said. "I would have never noticed that. It looked like it was part of the trailer. Can you find treasure with your goggles?"

Sammy considered this and shrugged. "I don't see why not. Er... after some updates."

"What about Gar—?" I froze. I'd almost said 'gargoyles.' I didn't want these kids to think I was crazy by asking about imaginary monsters.

"Gars?" Suzy asked. "Those are salt-water fish. You won't find any around here."

I pretended that I knew that. "Oh, yeah, heh, heh. I thought we were closer to the ocean." Then I shrugged. "I'm not from around here."

After an awkward silence, I finally asked, "So, where are you guys headed?"

"We came to see Mazy," said Suzy. "Your uncle doesn't mind."

"But how did you get back there?" I asked, nodding my head towards the woods.

Sammy said, "On the blacktop road, past your uncle's farm is a subdivision. We both live in it. There's a trail at the back that cuts through the woods and leads to that field back there."

We walked back towards the barn, talking. I was beginning to wish I had some neat friends like this back at my old school. At least some kids that did something other than make fart noises with their armpits or shot spit wads from straws.

Soon we came to a corral off the back of the barn. An old saggy horse was standing in it beneath a shade tree. I still didn't see any sign of my uncle (or Kat) so we all stood on the bottom rail of the wooden fence and fed clover to Mazy. We talked about our schools. I didn't say anything about the museum incident. Or the swarm of grasshoppers. Or the gargoyles. Or the ghost-tentacle things. So... I pretty much let them do all the talking.

I jumped down to pick some more clover. When I did, I saw Gertrude come running around the side of the barn.

She was barking like crazy and running fast.

UNCLE HORACE
GOES MISSING

"Hey Gerty," I said. "What's wrong, girl?"
She came straight at me.

"Gerty?"

She wasn't slowing down.

"Whoa girl!" I shouted. "WHOA!"

CRASH!

She plowed straight into me.

"Ooof!" I said, sprawling onto the grass. "Gerty, what—?"

She grabbed my sleeve in her mouth and tugged on it.

"She wants you to follow her," Suzy said. "Animals, especially dogs, are very attuned to human needs and ailments. Come on. Let's see what's wrong."

We all ran towards the house. Gerty was in the lead, barking her head off. She ran up the porch steps and through the open screen door. I went up the steps and stopped on the porch. To my surprise, I could see Grimlo through the big front window. He was standing on a table, cluttered with junk, looking out. His stone face looked worried. Now I was sure I hadn't dreamt the monsters from last night.

Just then Kat came running up and jumped over the flowerbed and landed on the porch railing. She clung there just like a ninja. "What's all the commotion?" Then she saw Suzy and said, "Oh, what are *you* doing here?"

There was a funny sound in her voice. I'd heard other girls in my school with the same sound. It wasn't exactly friendly.

Suzy walked up the steps and held up her magnifying glass towards Kat, like she was examining another bug. Then she turned to Sammy and said, "What's *she* doing here?"

Sammy quickly put his goggles back down and began typing commands into his controller. I could hear the whirring of his laptop from the porch. He was examining the situation in his own unique, cyborg way.

I didn't have time to wonder what the girls meant by their questions. Looking at the group of kids I said, "Uhh... I think I'd better handle this by myself. Wait right here."

And I ran inside and closed the front door.

Inside the house, Gerty was already sleeping, curled up on an old rug in the corner. The hourglasses were still running, but some were now upside down. One hourglass was laying sideways, but somehow the sand still moved from one side to the other.

"Uncle Horace?" I called. "Are you in here?"

"He ain't here, boy," Grimlo said. "That's why I sent Gerty to fetch ya."

"Where is he?" I said, pacing the front room. "What's wrong?"

"Arrr, it's a turr-able thing that's happened." Grimlo looked at the floor and shook his stone head.

"What happened?" I asked.

"It's horrible turr-able," Grimlo continued. "In all my live-long days, I never thought this would happen."

"What?"

"It's so turr-able I just don't know—"

"GRIMLO!" I yelled. "WHAT. HAPPENED?"

"Oh!" Grimlo said, looking surprised. "You ain't got to holler so. Your uncle's gone missin'."

I stood there dumbfounded with my mouth hanging open. How could he go missing? I just saw him last night. I still needed to find out about Mom. And who was going to train me now?

"Spickelark hole," Grimlo said, and slapped his hand under his chin.

I snapped my mouth shut, then clamped my hands to my head.

"Are you sure?" I asked, pacing the room. "I haven't seen him all morning, but there was a fire burning in his den fireplace just a few hours ago."

Grimlo nodded and moaned.

"Maybe he went to town?" I asked.

Grimlo shook his head and moaned sideways.

"Maybe he's taking a nap somewhere?"

Grimlo moaned louder, as if this idea was more horrible than the last.

I questioned him over and over as to where my uncle could have gone. Each idea caused Grimlo to moan louder than before.

Then I saw something even worse than hearing my uncle was missing. I saw the kids outside, staring at me through the big front window. There was Kat, perched on the porch railing like a spider-monkey, trying to see who I was talking to. Suzy had her magnifying glass up to the window. And Sammy was fidgeting with his space goggles. His giant, magnified eyes scanning the room.

My mouth fell open even wider.

Seeing my surprise, Grimlo turned around on the table and now saw the kids for the first time.

They were staring back at him.

FOUND OUT

"AHH!" yelled Grimlo at the giant eyes, and fell backwards off the table.

"AHH!" yelled Sammy when he saw the garden gnome's face move. He fell over backwards on the porch.

"AHH!" yelled Suzy, who dropped her magnifying glass.

"Awesome!" said Kat, who stood up on the rail to lean closer to the window.

Gerty slept through the commotion and snored gently from the corner.

BOING! Grimlo popped up like a spring and landed back on the table just as the front door swung open. One by one, the kids came stumbling in, gathering at the entryway to the front room. They stared in amazement.

"Oh, hey guys," I said. "Do you want to come in?" I glanced at Grimlo, who stood silently on the table.

"Uhh… what's everyone looking at?" I asked.

Sammy pushed the googles to the top of his head. "What was that thing you were talking to?"

I tried to sound surprised. I didn't want these kids thinking I always talked to inanimate objects.

"Thing?" I said.

"Come on, Milo," Kat said. "We all saw you talking to someone. Then that creepy gremlin turned around and looked at us. What is it, a robot? How do you control it?"

"Creepy gremlin?" Grimlo said from the table. Then he jumped down.

WHAM!

And the whole house shook.

"Aarrr!" Grimlo said as he moved across the floor. "Ya insult me again, and I be bitin' yer ankles off, I will!"

Everyone screamed and picked up their feet, dancing around as Grimlo made gnashing sounds with his mouth.

Chomp! Chomp! Chomp! Echoed through the house.

"It'll be turr-able, it will! Pain and agony of magnormous… uhh… gigantious… er… pain and agony!"

Chomp!

"Grimlo, stop!" I said. "It's OK, she didn't mean anything by it."

"It talks?" Suzy asked.

"And moves?" said Sammy.

"Can it swear?" Kat leaned forward, staring down at Grimlo.

Grimlo looked up at Kat with that one-eyed sideways look he'd given me the night before. "Arrr… you dim, girl?" he said. "I'm a garden gnome. Of course I can swear! Try this one on for size."

"No! No!" I interrupted. "I think we can skip that for now, Grimlo." I looked around at their stunned faces and laughed a little. "He's quite the kidder, Grimlo is."

"Arrr... you sure?" Grimlo whispered to me, as we walked back towards the table. "Not even a little '*by Blackbeard's toejam*'?"

BOING! He hopped back up on the table.

"Uhh... maybe later," I said to him.

I turned to the group and said, "Grimlo, this is Kat, Sammy and Suzy." Pointing at each one. "Everyone, this is Grimlo."

Grimlo pulled out his stone pipe, already lit, and took a big puff. He eyed each kid as they crept a bit closer, trying to figure out how the garden gnome was moving and talking. Sammy inspected Grimlo with his goggles on, then off. Then he'd make an adjustment on his controller, then goggles on, goggles off. Suzy flipped through her reference guide, looking for an explanation. Kat just rubbed her chin and glared suspiciously at him.

Finally, just as they got a little too close, Grimlo blew a large cloud of smoke at them, pushing them back. A low growl rumbled out of him that vibrated down to the floor. That was his way of saying they'd gotten close enough.

"Well," I said, looking at Grimlo, then back at the group. "I guess I need to tell you a bit about myself and what I saw last night."

Thirty minutes later, I had finished telling them about the strange mist, and the moving clouds, the gargoyle face, and of course, meeting Grimlo. Normally, people wouldn't believe such a thing, but the fact that a cement garden gnome sat smoking a pipe on the living room table, was kind of hard to ignore.

Amazingly, Gerty had woken up at some point during my story, and not noticing the kids, had wandered off down the hall.

When I'd finished, I leaned back in my chair, exhausted. It

felt like I'd been talking all day, but it was just after noon. Then I suddenly remembered why we were here.

"My uncle!" I said, sitting up. "Grimlo, what happened to Uncle Horace?"

"Ay, we need to get to that, don't we?" he said. "But before we do, maybe a bite to eat would settle yer stomachs. It's a bit of a tale."

We followed him down the hall, surprised to see a plate of ham and cheese sandwiches sitting on the middle of the kitchen table. There were bowls of chips and apples, also. Four glasses of iced tea sat at four different place settings.

Grimlo had sprung up to a small bay window that stuck out the back wall of the kitchen. The window was crowded with herbs in pots that hung down from the ceiling. The plants reached for sunlight, casting spooky tentacle-shadows onto the floor.

He walked back and forth slowly, puffing his pipe, as if thinking about how to start. When the crunching of apples and potato chips had gone quiet, we all turned our chairs to listen.

Then he told us an unbelievable story.

GARGOYLES
EXPLAINED
(...SORT OF)

"Your Uncle Horace is a Gargoyle Hunter, Milo," Grimlo began. "I expect you knew that. There are very few on this continent. For now, at least." And he gave me a look that said he expected something from me.

"He's also the guardian of the Midday Gate and Keeper of the Moonstone."

"The what?" we all said in unison.

A wistful look came over Grimlo's stone face, as if he were remembering a wonderful time, long, long ago. "Every year on the first full moon after the summer solstice, the Dance of the Gargoyles occurs."

"The summer what?" I asked.

"The summer solstice is the longest day of the year," Suzy said. "In terms of daylight, anyway."

"Ayy, she's right," Grimlo said.

"And some cultures consider it the start of their new year," Suzy said. "But what is the Dance of the Gargoyles and what does it have to do with the full moon?"

"The Dance of the Gargoyles is a *palaver* in a way, a meetin' of the great gargoyle clans. By the magic light of the first full moon, which is called the Gargoyle Moon, they air their grievances and discuss worldly events and how to fulfill their solemn oaths."

"What solemn oaths?" Sammy asked. His goggles were back on, and his huge eyeballs blinked at Grimlo.

Grimlo shivered. "Eewww... those eyeballs... Anywho, their solemn oath is to protect the human race, of course."

"Protect the human race?" I said. "I thought gargoyles were mean and evil... or something like that."

Grimlo shook his head. "No, that there is a falsehood, what you'd call a Miss Carrot Rightzation, from those Hollywood director types. Run amuck, they have."

I knew he meant to say, *mischaracterization*, but stayed quiet.

Then he knocked his pipe against his head and whispered. "Californy sun cooked their noodles."

Aahhh.... We all nodded our understanding.

"Anyhow, a gargoyle's sworn oath is to protect the human race. It's all there in the bylaws. But gargoyles are an ornery bunch—bad tempered, most of the time—and tricky-tricky."

He pointed the end of his pipe at us to emphasize how tricky they were.

"The ones in the good clans ain't much trouble, and they abide by the laws well enough. But some of 'em..." Grimlo shivered.

"Woo-ooo, some of 'em are meaner than Spickelark hens hoardin' Burrberries!"

He nodded at us like we should know what that meant.

"That's right. And the mean ones are always escapin'. That's why we got to have Gargoyle Hunters. But one of 'em…"

He trailed off and looked at each one of us with something like concern in his eyes. At that moment, I thought he was genuinely afraid for us.

"What?" I asked. "What about one of them?"

"One of the clans is downright deadly."

We all sat quietly for a moment, looking at each other. Then Kat spoke up. "But what about the Midday Gate? And the Moonstone?"

"Oh, Blackbeard!" Grimlo said. "I almost forgot the most important part; we'll talk about the gate later. Milo's uncle is the Keeper of the Moonstone. And there's only one Keeper on this whole continent. It's his job to protect the Moonstone. Without it, and performin' the proper rituals of course, the gargoyles can't palaver, and if the gargoyles can't palaver, they can't protect the human race—blah, blah, and fair thee well!"

Sammy finally spoke up. "So let me see if I have this straight. Milo's uncle protects the Moonstone. The Moonstone protects the gargoyles. The gargoyles protect us."

Grimlo shrugged his shoulders and said, "It's more like the Moonstone *controls* the gargoyles. You can't just call a bunch of gargoyles to a secret meetin' and expect them all to behave!"

"Why not?" Sammy asked.

"Arrr… you dim, boy?" Grimlo asked. "Why not? Because there

could be pandemonium. That's why not. There could be calamity. There could be gamblin'. THERE. COULD. BE. KARAOKE!"

All of us kids looked at each other.

"Karaoke?" I said. "What's scary about that?"

Grimlo gave me his sideways-bird look. "Have you ever heard a gargoyle try to sing?"

I shook my head. "No. But it can't be that bad. Can it?"

Grimlo coughed twice to clear his throat. Then he sang:

"Wee aarre the chamm-pions."

We clamped our hands over our ears. His voice sounded like giant boulders crashing down a mountain.

"WEEE AAARRRE THE CHAAAMM-PIONS!"

"OK! OK! STOP!" I said. "We get it. Don't we, guys?" I looked around. Everyone was nodding, but still had their hands over their ears.

"Karaoke would be bad," I said to Grimlo. "Very bad."

Grimlo seemed disappointed that we didn't want him to continue singing. He nodded and stuck his hands in his pockets.

"But what about the Moonstone?" I asked.

"Arrr... without the Moonstone, the gargoyles could escape."

MORE GARGOYLE STUFF

"And how do they escape?" I asked.

Grimlo pulled a pipe from the inside of his vest and puffed on it. "Each stone gargoyle has a spirit inside of it. That's part of their solemn oath—they must stand guard for all time in the stone body they're given."

He looked at each one of us to see that we understood. Then he continued.

"But once a year, when the summer solstice is approaching, the Moonstone wakes up and draws the gargoyles to its location. To humans, it looks like the gargoyles are still attached to the buildings or churches, or wherever they are stationed. But in reality, their focus, and spirit, goes to where the Moonstone is."

"So, the Moonstone creates something like an electric fence?" Kat asked. "Like to keep your dogs in the yard. Only it keeps them in and other things out?"

"For the most part," said Grimlo.

"And without the Moonstone, there would be no electric fence?" Kat said.

"In a way."

At this point, I wasn't overly confident that the Moonstone did much of anything, but I didn't say that.

"So what does the stone look like?" Kat asked.

"The Moonstone is about the size of a Borker egg," said Grimlo, holding out his hands.

"A what?" asked Suzy. "A Borker egg?"

"Yeah, a Borker egg," Grimlo replied. "You know... a Borker..." He nodded as if this would help Suzy understand.

She shook her head.

"No?"

"No."

"Well," Grimlo said, "it's uh... er..." Then pointed at Sammy's head. "About that size! Only, you know, egg shape."

Sammy's huge eyes blinked back at us in confusion. "Who, me?" he said quietly.

Grimlo waved him off and continued. "Anywho, it's crystal blue and silvery with dark veins runnin' through it. Whoever controls the Moonstone, controls the gargoyles, in a way. If that person wanted to let the gargoyles go free, they could do that. But then there'd be no more protection for humans.

"If that person wanted to take the stone to a city and call the gargoyles, they could do it. Then, if they released the gargoyles from their solemn oaths, there'd be havoc in that city. That's why the stone is kept out here, on a faraway mountain. There's plenty of room for the gargoyles to palaver in privacy. And little chance that something could go wrong.

"Milo's uncle knows the secret to the stone—how it must be used before, during and after the Dance of the Gargoyles. You see, there are vurry specific things that must be done with it. And if the steps ain't followed just right…"

Grimlo shook his head like something bad would happen.

"But I already saw a gargoyle," I said. "And it's not a full moon yet. How is that possible?"

"The gargoyle chiefs can arrive anytime they want. It's in their power. Sometimes they have business of a more private matter to attend to before all the others arrive. But on the night of the full moon, that's when it's important that yer Uncle Horace be on his toes. He has to work the ritual just right."

"Which one did I see?" I asked. I jumped up to explain. "Man, was it scary! It had giant wings and a big ugly face, with fangs. Must have been ten feet tall, maybe twenty. And ugly, too. Did I mention that? It was probably one of the mean ones and tried to escape and my uncle went to go catch it and—"

Grimlo cleared his throat.

He looked at me just like my teacher does when I talk too loud in class. So I knew to sit down.

"Arrrr… you quite finished?" Grimlo said.

"Oh, sorry," I said. Then I whispered to the kids, "It was just kind of ugly."

Grimlo continued. "You, young Milo, made a not-so-great first impression on Goji of the Gargouille clan, the oldest gargoyle clan in existence today!"

"Oh," I said, in a rather small voice.

"Goji is not only the chief of that clan, but is also the High Justice."

Uh… I was beginning to feel a little sick.

"And the High Justice decides ALL THINGS regarding gargoyle law," Grimlo continued.

I mean, I really think my ham sandwich was bad. I was beginning to sweat.

"Includin' interactions with and pertainin' to—Gargoyle Hunters!"

Oh, man!

Uugghh… I sank back in my chair. Sweat rolled off my forehead. I looked around the room. Suzy, Sammy and Kat all stared back at me silently. Their eyes wide with alarm.

"He wasn't really that ugly," I said, weakly. "Kinda handsome, actually."

"Your sneakin' into that field last night was a serious breach of etiquette," Grimlo continued. "I spent half the night explaining to Goji how you ain't been trained proper yet, and that you'd learn right fast. That way he'd give you another chance."

I sat up, surprised. "Really? You did that for me?"

Grimlo gave a slight nod of his head.

"Wow," I said. "Thanks." And my hands did their little happy dance.

"Arrr… don't mention it."

Sammy gave me a funny look when my hands went crazy, but

didn't say anything. He adjusted his goggles and began typing something into his controller.

"But what about Milo's uncle?" Suzy asked. "What happened to him?"

"Yeah," I said. "What about Uncle Horace?"

Grimlo began pacing on the windowsill, hands behind his back.

"That's a more serious matter," he said. "I'm afraid he's been kidnapped."

"Kidnapped?" I said. "Why would anyone want to kidnap an old uncle?"

"Remember, he ain't just an old uncle," Grimlo said. "He's the Keeper of the Moonstone. He knows its secrets."

Ah… finally, I thought. *That's what the stone warrior was trying to tell me in the museum. The secret is about the Moonstone. But what?*

Kat spoke up. "And he protects the Moonstone, which protects the gargoyles."

Then Sammy said, "And the gargoyles protect us!"

"Ayyy," Grimlo said.

"But who would want to kidnap him?" Suzy asked.

Grimlo's face grew serious. "The Snarloks."

THE SNARLOKS

"The Snarlok clan is the second oldest clan in existence today," Grimlo said.

"Excuse me," said Suzy. "You described Goji's clan the same way. You said, 'in existence today.' Does that mean there are even older clans that no longer exist? Like, they've died or something?"

"Ayyy, it does," said Grimlo. "The histories of the Great Old Ones have been lost. There are giant gargoyles all around the world that have gone silent. That's one of the mysteries that Goji and the other chiefs have been tryin' to unravel. But we're talkin' about the Snarloks.

"Silas is the chief of the Snarlok clan. No one knows how he was created or where his stones lie."

"Wait," said Sammy. He'd taken his space goggles off, so his eyes were normal sized now, but his hair was matted down in places, making his head look lopsided. "What does that mean, 'where his stones lie'?"

"Every gargoyle must have an anchor, a body, where their spirit can live. We call it, 'where their stones lie.' It's like their home and is typically attached to castles, churches or other buildings. But for Silas, no one knows where that is. It's rumored that he once protected a great island in the farthest reaches of the oceans. A place no one could sail to, and where a monster even greater than Silas lived. But one day a great earthquake sank the island, and its location was lost to history. But Silas survived."

"How do you know he survived?" asked Suzy.

"He used to appear at the most important gargoyle meetings. He was the High Justice of the gargoyle clans in the long-ago days."

"The High Justice?" I said. "But I thought that was Goji?"

"Ayyy, it is. Now. Silas didn't want the gargoyles to protect the humans. He wanted to enslave them! He wanted to use his eternal life to protect whatever monstrosity he served on that mysterious island. Some creature rumored to not even be from this world.

"So, there was a great battle between Goji and Silas. It was a fearful thing, I've heard. When Goji won, he banished Silas and the entire Snarlok clan. And the Snarloks have never forgotten, and they'll never stop trying to take over the other clans."

We all sat there in stunned silence. Finally, Kat said, "And if Silas takes over the clans, it'll be bad for us humans, won't it?"

"Ayyy, vurry bad, indeed."

Something had just occurred to me, and I had a sinking feeling in my stomach. I thought back to the day in the museum. "What do the Snarloks look like?" I asked Grimlo.

"Arrr... the ugliest things that's ever been dreamed of by man. The legend is that Silas was created in the image of the monster he served, and has the hulking body of a man, with claws on his feet and hands. But because of the strange island where the monster lived, or mayhap because it sunk beneath the waves, Silas has the head of an octopus with a beak-mouth strong enough to crack a human skull. Worse than that, he has long red tentacles growin' out of his back, with suckers all over them. Over time, all the Snarloks have transformed into something just as ugly. But the common feature is the long red tentacles. No other gargoyle clan has that."

I looked at the other kids and tried to swallow, but my throat was dry. I was pretty sure that Grimlo had just described the red ghost tentacles that had attacked me and Mom just a few days ago.

If that was true, it meant the Snarloks already knew who I was.

A FRIEND
IN NEED

"So, what do we do now?" asked Kat.

"We?" said Grimlo. "There ain't nothin' can be done by you kids. That would be an even worse breach of etiquette, not to mention, you couldn't even get into the gargoyle mist without—"

He stopped as if he'd said too much.

Kat said, "But we have to help Milo find his uncle. He can't do it alone. He's not even from around here."

"Yeah," said Sammy.

Suzy nodded in agreement.

I spoke up. "Uh… thanks guys, but I… well… it's not your problem and…"

I thought about Mom. I really missed her and wished she was here right now. She'd know what to do. I looked down at my hands and thought about the last time we'd talked. It was at our own kitchen table. We sat around it, just like we were doing now. But I didn't feel lonely or scared then.

Suddenly, I felt something in my eye. I jumped up and walked down the hall to wipe it away. I heard the others whispering as I went.

I sat on the steps of the front porch and looked up at the hill. If only I hadn't gone out there last night. Maybe Uncle Horace would still be here. And if he was still here, he'd be able to tell me about Mom and none of this would have happened. Trouble again, I thought. The special Milo Savage kind.

I heard the screen door creak open. "Hey, Milo," Sammy said. "Are you OK?"

"Yeah." My voice squeaked. I coughed to clear it. "Yeah," I said louder. "I'm fine. What's up?"

"Well... Grimlo said this was an important part, and that you should probably hear it."

I sighed. "OK." I got up and followed him back down the hall.

I sat in the same kitchen chair. Grimlo stood on the windowsill. His pipe was tucked away inside his jacket. He put his hands behind him and leaned way back, stretching. We heard the snap, crackle and pop of his spine. It sounded like ice cubes cracking in a glass after you poured warm soda on them.

Kat spoke up. "Grimlo, you started to say something about the mist. What did you mean?"

"The problem with finding Milo's uncle is complicated," said Grimlo. "He's in the mist, you see. And gettin' *into* the mist is the first problem. But I'm afraid that's where the problems start, not end."

"What does that mean, *getting into the mist*?" Sammy asked.

"No one that ain't a Gargoyle Hunter can enter the gargoyle

realm. And to get into the gargoyle realm, you must be able to enter the mist. That's where the gate is hidden. The realm is the most likely place where the Snarloks have hidden his uncle. But fer the life of me, I don't know how the Snarloks got back in."

"The mist," I said. "I saw it last night on the hill. You mean that was magic mist or something?"

"Not magic exactly," said Grimlo. "But to normal folks, it just looks like regular fog. They can't see what's movin' around inside it. Oh, sometimes people get a glimpse of something movin', or think they do. Those people may have a way-back ancestor who had a bit of hunter-magic in them, but that don't make 'em a Gargoyle Hunter. Anyway, normal folks can't see what's in the mist, and more important, they can't go into it. They walk right through it and come out on the other side of the field. But Milo, when you walked into the mist, you were going *into* the world of the gargoyles, without knowin' it."

"So that's how I saw Goji."

"Ayup."

"So…" I said slowly. "That means I'm the only one who can save my uncle." The words seemed to hang in the air, echoing in the quiet kitchen. My stomach sank.

Grimlo nodded.

"But you said that Milo hasn't been trained up yet," said Kat. "He can't go by himself."

"Yeah," Sammy chimed in. "He almost got himself squooshed already. He doesn't even know the protocols!"

Sammy smiled and nodded at me like he was really trying to

help. But I was feeling kind of crummy that everyone thought I couldn't do anything right. I mean, I had already survived a Snarlok attack after all and—

"Hey, wait a minute," I said. "The Snarloks have already tried to get me, twice."

Then I quickly told them about the episode with the stone warrior in the museum and the ghost tentacles at my house.

"And I didn't have this in the museum." I pulled the multicolored stone from beneath my shirt. It twisted slowly at the end of its leather strap. The metal braiding glinted in the afternoon light, but the stone stayed dark. In fact, the multiple colors were almost gone. It looked rather ominous compared to the first time I'd seen it.

Grimlo eyed me sideways again. "You survived a Snarlok attack, with nary any trainin', and not even a talisman?"

I nodded, then said, "Well, my mom helped some... a lot actually. But in the museum, I was by myself."

Grimlo scratched his stone head beneath his hat. A loud grating noise echoed through the kitchen that made my teeth vibrate.

He nodded again, then said, "Mayhap, there's somethin' can be done. But Goji won't abide with an untrained hunter roamin' around in his world. Not without a proper escort." Here, he nodded his head and spit on the floor, as if to make the idea final. Even his spit made a loud *Kathunk!* sound when it hit the wood.

"Alright," Grimlo said. "I knows what needs to be done. Come with me."

WE FORM
A CLAN

Back in the front room Grimlo was rummaging through the drawers of a large bureau. "I know those darn things arrrr somewhere. Gerty!" he called. "Where are the—"

Suddenly Gerty came trotting down the steps. She was wearing a vest. It looked like the adventurer's vest that Suzy had on—tan, with a lot of pockets—only made for a big shaggy dog. In her mouth she carried a stone box. It was like the box my mom had in the kitchen, only a different color.

She set it on the coffee table next to the sundial, then went over to her rug in the corner of the room. Instead of falling asleep, she sat up (like a regular dog) and looked at Grimlo. She was waiting for something.

"You're the best, Gerty," Grimlo said.

BOING! He sprang up onto the coffee table, but this time landed as light as a feather. He didn't make a sound. Weird!

"Now, this ain't never been tried before," Grimlo said. "So, it may end horrible-like for all of ya', but…" And then he scratched his head again. "Well... we'll just have to see what happens."

See what happens? I thought. That didn't sound very promising.

Then he pressed the corner of the stone box and a loud, grating sound filled the house. It sounded like a mountain groaning.

"OW!" we all yelled, covering our ears.

"Oh, sorry, sorry," Grimlo said. "Shoulda warned ya. This here box has been closed for so long, wasn't sure it was gonna open without a good kick!"

As the lid of the box settled open, the grating sounds of stone faded. For a moment, nothing happened. Then, a faint, bluish glow rose out of the box.

"Milo," whispered Suzy. "Your shirt."

I looked at my shirt. Beneath it, the same weird, blue glow was coloring the material. I could feel it begin to pulse, almost like a heartbeat.

Grimlo reached into the box, and pulled out three rawhide necklaces, similar to mine. Each one held a small stone of different color. But they all glowed with the same blue light.

He looked at each one of us, like he was thinking about changing his mind. Then he looked at Gerty. I thought I saw a slight nod of her head.

He held out a necklace to each of the kids. One by one, they stepped up, took one, then stood at their own spot around the coffee table.

Grimlo said, "These here stones, just like the one that Milo has, are fragments from the original Moonstone. It got chipped during the great war between Goji and Silas. These pieces were passed down to the Keeper of the Moonstone, to be used in its protection.

"Horace had them made into these here necklaces for just such ah 'mergency. Each one is a talisman. And a talisman will help whoever wears it enter the gargoyle realm. You must protect them like you would the Moonstone, because if a Snarlok gets ahold of one of these, it would be vurry bad. But don't worry, no Snarlok can take a talisman off you, if you don't want 'em to. It's not in their power. At least, not while yer livin'... so there's that."

Then, almost as an afterthought, he said, "But if you got squooshed to smithereens, then they'd be able to take it, or if some other terrible fate befalls you..."

"Uh, we get the point," I said.

We all looked at each other. I touched my own talisman with my fingers. It was glowing brighter now, and the other three stones seemed to pulse in unison with mine.

"If you put these on," Grimlo said, "you'll be a clan. Like a family. You'll help each other, and with a good guide, your wits, and a bit of good luck, you'll find Horace and bring him back."

We looked at each other and nodded.

"So, each of you put your talismans on," Grimlo said.

Each person slipped the rock necklace over their heads. When they did, the stones stopped pulsing, and shone with a steady light.

"Join hands."

We did, but thankfully we were already standing boy, girl, boy, girl. Even then, I hadn't expected my summer adventure to include holding hands with two girls I'd just met.

"On this historic day, I declare you the Savage Clan!" Grimlo said. "The first clan of gargoyle hunters granted the authority to enter the gargoyle realm in protection of the Moonstone. May you succeed in your quest, without getting squooshed to smithereens!"

Oh man, I thought. Grimlo could have left off the part about getting squooshed to smithereens.

And just like that, the stones stopped glowing, and the room fell silent.

"So, what now?" asked Suzy. "Who's going to be our guide?"

Then we all heard a new voice, like a sweet English aunt, from the corner of the room. "Well, I am of course, love," said Gerty.

GERTY'S
SURPRISE

"Gerty can talk?" we all said in unison.

Then we swarmed her, petting her and ruffling her ears. We'd never seen a talking dog before and couldn't help ourselves. And to be honest, we'd never seen a talking garden gnome either, but didn't think Grimlo would appreciate us patting his head.

"Now, now," she said. "Watch the paws please."

"But I don't understand," I said. "Earlier, by the barn, why didn't you just tell me Uncle Horace was gone instead of knocking me down and almost dragging me here?"

Gerty stood up and shook her head and body, like a dog does. She sent shaggy hair floating up into the air. "Oh, I am sorry about that, Milo. But I do get excited when I'm out and about. It's as if my legs get full of energy and just don't want to stop."

Man, I knew how that felt, I thought, rubbing my hands together.

"And as far as not telling you, well, humans can only understand me here in the house, or at night, of course. It's like that for all of us."

Then I remembered that Flick the cat and Grimlo had both spoken to me last night after dark.

Gerty walked to the other side of the coffee table and stood behind Grimlo. "But I've been here at your uncle's house for a long time, and have journeyed with him into the realm on several occasions. It makes sense for me to be your guide. I'm very good with remembering my way."

That explained how she led me to my room so easily, down the maze of halls. That, and the fact that she's lived here for a long time, but it was all starting to make sense.

I still wasn't sure who had been making our food though, but thought I'd ask about that later.

"Aarrright, aright," Grimlo said. "Enough pollywaggin'! We got to get you armed up. Then I got to adjust this infernal machine."

"'Armed up'?" Sammy asked. His space goggles were back on, and he blinked giant eyelids at Grimlo.

Grimlo shivered. "Ewww... I'm gonna need a whole flask of grog to forget those giant peepers."

BOINGG! Grimlo sprung off the floor, bounced off the cushions of the antique couch, skipped off the arm of a wingback chair and bounced higher still. Suddenly, it looked like he was floating in midair, right in front of the bow and arrow set that hung on the wall. It must have been my imagination because I was pretty sure he couldn't fly. But just as quickly as he sprung up there, he had the bow and arrows in his hands, and landed back on the floor.

WHAM! The whole room shook.

Grimlo handed the bow and arrows to Kat, bowed slightly to

her, then said, "May yer aim be true and yer feathers... uh... may yer feathers stay... uh... Oh, Blackbeard! Don't let yer feathers fall out!"

Kat took the bow and arrow and bowed. "Wow, thanks!" A mischievous grin crossed her face.

Then Gerty walked to the old bookshelf stuffed with books and maps. She stood on her hind legs and sniffed around on a high shelf. Suddenly, she let out a giant sneeze, *AACHHOOO!* And a large cloud of dust flew into the air. "Oh, there it is," she said.

She came down with a small, leather-bound book in her mouth. Then she handed it to Suzy. "In a time of need, may you find the answer you seek."

Impressed onto the leather cover were these words: *Field Guide to Gargoyles and Stuff.* Suzy bowed slightly and said, "Thank you."

Grimlo had already done his bouncing trick again, plucking a set of the weird looking goggles off the wall. He tossed them to Sammy. "Here ya aarrrr goggle-boy. Don't fall in a hole."

Sammy caught the goggles, then bowed and said, "Wow, thanks, Grimlo!"

Grimlo shuffled his feet a bit as if he was embarrassed by how happy Sammy was for the gift. "Eh... don't mention it." He pulled out his pipe, took a big puff and said, "Now, fer the task at hand—"

"Wait," said Suzy. "What about Milo? Doesn't he get anything?"

"Yeah," said Kat, "like a flame-thrower or something?" She held out her quiver of arrows and made a loud sound with her mouth, like she was burning up the Snarloks.

PWOOSH!

Then Sammy chimed in, "Or maybe laser-beam eyes!" Then put his hands next to his eyes and waggled his two pointer fingers.

BBZZZZ! BBZZZZ! "I kill you with my laser-beam eyes!" he said in a robot voice.

Kat pointed at Sammy. *PWOOSH!*

Sammy pointed at Kat. *BBZZZZ!*

PWOOSH!

BBZZZZ!

Grimlo's voice went squeaky high. "A flame-thrower? Laser-beam eyes? Against gargoyles?"

Then he raised his foot and with one giant stomp, slammed it on the floor, rocking the house on its foundation. All four of us flew up in the air when the floor buckled. The furniture bounced up several inches, the coffee table danced around on each of its four legs, even the dust flew up in the air again. We landed with hard thuds on the floor. Miraculously, everything else landed right back in its original spot and nothing broke.

"Aarrr… you finished?" said Grimlo. He looked at us sternly and we understood that joke-time was over. When we all nodded, he continued. "Milo's got what he needs. Mayhap he don't know it yet, but it's in there somewhere." And he tapped his pipe against his head.

"Fer your sakes, here's to hopin' he can figure it out. Now. Here's the plan."

A VERY STRANGE CLOCK

We listened to Grimlo's plan, then looked at Gerty. She sat calmly like she was waiting to go on her afternoon walk. Nothing in her demeanor said she was about to lead a bunch of kids (even if we were a clan) into the mystical world of the gargoyles.

Grimlo's plan consisted of Gerty leading us into the gargoyle realm. There, we were to make our way to Goji's platform. He would give us a clue as to where we would possibly find my uncle. Then all we had to do was solve the clue, find him, avoid offending any gargoyles, and make our way back out.

What could go wrong?

I looked at the clocks on the walls. One of them was shaped like a large owl. Its black wood was intricately carved and tufts of feathers, like horns, stuck up from the head. Its feet were carved into great claws that gripped a thick branch. Where the owls face should have been was the face of an old clock. Its clock hands displayed that it was 4:15.

All the other clocks showed different times, and I wondered

how anyone could tell the real time in this house. But it was so light out, it was easy to know that evening was still hours away, and I wondered how Gerty could lead us if she could only speak in the house or when it was dark.

"Now, to adjust this infernal machine," Grimlo said.

BOINGG!

He sprung up to an hourglass mounted on a wall. The hourglasses were all held by metal brackets mounted to the walls. The brackets sort of looked like sconces, the things that held torches to the walls of castles. Each hourglass could be tilted upside down, by spinning it on an axis held by the bracket.

As Grimlo sprung up before the different hourglasses, he adjusted each one differently. Some were turned upside down, where all the sand sat at the top, some were tilted sideways, and the sand stopped running, and a few were tilted just a little, one way or the other.

Then he sprung down to the coffee table and stooped over the sundial. He looked at the shadow that lay across the faceplate, then cocked his head and looked at the owl clock on the wall. It showed that it was now 4:19. He was checking the time on the sundial.

"Hey, wait a minute," I said. "We're inside."

Grimlo looked up at me slowly, one stone eyebrow raised in concern. "Vurry, observant," he said. Then he looked at the others. "Nothin' to worry about there!" Then he twirled his finger by his head like I was crazy.

"I know we're inside," I said. "I mean, how is the sundial casting a shadow? The sun isn't shining through the window, and if the shadow is being made from the lamp light, it won't be the right time."

Grimlo stood up and cracked his back. He was smiling. He took his pipe out and gave it a long puff. "Vurry good, Milo." Then he tapped his head with his pipe. "Keep yer wits about ya' and you'll do fine. Now, as far as the shadow goes—"

He pointed the end of his pipe to the ceiling above the sundial. There hung the crazy chandelier I'd seen last night. The light bulbs were off, but the showerhead thing with the glass dome was glowing.

"That there is the actual sunlight," Grimlo said. "There's a device on the roof that tracks the position of the sun. It captures its light and funnels it down a long tube. The sunlight comes out of that glass dome. Your uncle invented it."

"And the sundial tells the correct time?" Suzy asked.

"Never off by a second," said Grimlo. "But it does more than that. Watch this."

Then he bent over the sundial and grabbed the gnomon, the triangular blade that sticks up and makes the shadow. He turned the gnomon. It made quiet ticking sounds, like the turning of a ratchet. He turned it slowly, glancing up at the owl clock.

"Hey!" Sammy yelled. "Look at that!"

He was pointing out the window.

We all ran to the big picture window that looked out across the front porch onto the yard. From this view, we could see Gargoyle Hill up to the left. Everything was getting darker.

"What's going on?" asked Suzy. "It's only 4:25 by my watch. And we're not supposed to have a solar eclipse today."

"Are there clouds?" asked Kat.

"Not a one," said Sammy. He'd put his goggles on to analyze the situation.

We heard the faint clicks of the gnomon as Grimlo continued turning it. A heavy mist began to settle over the hill. Long shadows crept out around the buildings. The forest began to darken. It was turning night.

"What's happening, Grimlo?" I asked. "How are you doing that?"

He turned a few more clicks, then stopped, but didn't let go. He was still holding the gnomon.

"That should be enough time," Grimlo said.

I noticed that the owl clock now sat at 11:59. One minute before midnight. It seemed to be in sync with the sundial. The other clocks still displayed odd times and hadn't changed.

"Now," said Grimlo, "you stick with Gerty. She knows where to start. You get yer job done. Then, you get back here, at least onto the porch, by the time that clock settles down."

Then he let go of the gnomon.

As soon as he did, the owl clock flapped its wings. Once. Twice. Then sprung off its carved branch and began to fly around the room!

WHOA! Super cool!

Although the owl clock was completely silent, a faint ticking sound could be heard coming from the gnomon. It was like a timer.

Grimlo sprung down and opened the front door. The dark of the night seemed to flood in and fill the room.

"Pip, pip," Gerty said. "Let's get a move on. We have a long way to go."

We all followed her out onto the front porch. Grimlo came last.

"Arrr... like I said, you keep together and follow Gerty. No tomfoolery either. And whatever you do, even if you can't find Horace, you get back onto this porch before that clock in there settles."

"Why?" I asked. "What happens if we don't get back before it settles?"

"Come along dears," Gerty said. "It's bad luck to start a journey on such a nasty thought."

And just like that, we headed for the mist.

INTO
THE MIST

We walked towards Gargoyle Hill. Thick clouds of mist rolled down it like ocean waves. For a moment, I thought the hill was trying to warn us away. When the waves of mist crossed the dry creek bed, they evaporated into soft tendrils. It was if an electric fence really did exist around this place and the mist burned itself up trying to get out. They reminded me of the ghost tentacles, and I suddenly had the feeling that this might not be a good idea.

Off to our right, the forest was black with gloom, dotted only by the old streetlamps. Everywhere I looked, there was a shadow darker than the last, trying to swallow up the light. Occasionally I caught a glimpse of something shimmering beyond the dark, and wondered if the Snarloks were hiding there, watching us.

"Now listen up," Gerty said. "When we cross the dry creek bed, we'll officially be on Gargoyle Hill, so everyone pay attention. And whatever you do, stay together!"

Suzy had been studying her new book with a small penlight. She stopped and looked at her watch. "I have an alarm set for three hours from now. I figure if we travel that long and still haven't found Milo's uncle, we can decide what to do, and still have three hours to get back. With some time to spare. It would only be 10:30 at that point."

"Good thinking," Sammy said. He had already fixed the new goggles over the top of his old ones and was twisting knobs like crazy. Now he looked like a mad inventor with miniature telescopes strapped to his face.

"What do you see?" I asked. "Any gargoyles?"

"Nothing yet," he said. "I don't know how they work."

We came to the place in the creek where I had crossed the night before. It wasn't very deep and was rather low on our side. The hill began to rise here, and the other side of the creek bed was about three feet higher. I shivered without knowing why. Just beyond this point was where I had almost gotten squooshed by Goji. I hoped he was in a better mood tonight.

Gerty clambered up the creek bank, which was crumbly dirt and rock. She sniffed the air, then turned and motioned for each of us to climb up. Kat went first, springing up the side almost as well as Grimlo did in the house. It must have been the ninja in her. Then Sammy tried, but his sneakers were untied and halfway up, he stepped on a string which caused him to slide back down, scraping his stomach on the rocks.

He sat at the bottom rubbing his stomach. "Oh, man. That hurts."

"Tie your shoes," Suzy said. "And for goodness sakes, take off your goggles when you climb."

"Good idea," Sammy said.

He finally made it up, then turned to help Suzy, but she proved to be good at climbing, finding handholds of roots and tough grasses to pull herself up.

I followed easily. When I stood up, I looked up the hill expecting to see a clan of gargoyles and saw…

Nothing.

I couldn't see a thing. Nada. Zip. Kaput. Except the mist of course, which was rolling fast at us. It was even thicker than it had been last night.

"Follow my trail," Gerty said. "Stay in a straight line and just follow my trail. The mist is a bit thick and will distort your voices, so don't rely on your ears."

"Yesss…" hissed a sly voice on our left. "You wouldn't want to get lossst," then the voice was on our right, "in here. It would be purrr-fectly awful."

Suddenly Flick's eyes appeared straight out of the mist in front of us. Two blue gemstones floated above a button nose. The strange thing was that they were five feet up in the air, as if he was sitting on something we couldn't see.

"Now Flick," Gerty said, "you behave. The dears have enough to think about without you prancing about causing mischief."

"But I so love an evening ssstrollll," said Flick. "I think I'll mee-ow-ander a bit."

And just like that, Flick was gone.

"Pay him no mind," Gerty said. "He's only off to chase field mice."

"Does he eat them?" Kat asked. Again, I thought I heard a strange anticipation in her question and imagined her eyes twinkling at the idea.

"Only the exotic ones," Gerty said. "Flick has a very discriminating palate."

We walked up and up, further than I had the night before. Faint lamplight far across the field.

How many lamps does this place have? I wondered.

Their lights cast a ghostly glow through the fog. They seemed to have been randomly placed across the field that sloped up the hill. This was strange because I hadn't noticed any lamps up here during the day.

The hill was big, and I thought we still had a long way to the top. Fortunately, Gerty's trail was easy to follow because the grass was stamped down by all the feet. Beads of water rolled down my face as we moved through the thick clouds.

Up ahead I saw the faint outline of a small building. It looked like an old well house; a building made of stone that covers a deep well. It was covered with vines and surrounded by tall weeds.

I followed Suzy (her vest mostly) and heard faint murmurs, but couldn't make out the words.

Gerty took a path directly toward the well house. Suddenly I remembered seeing the note on Uncle Horace's desk. The Well House was on my training list! It must be important. I hoped we were going in it.

A little further and the hill leveled out and Gerty stopped.

Wait, we can't be at the top already, I thought. We hadn't walked far enough. Besides, the well house was still up ahead somewhere in the mist.

Gerty turned around and said, "We're at the edge of the great gargoyle realm. It's imperative you only walk where I do until I say it's safe. There are booby traps along the paths."

What paths? I wondered. All I could see was the wet grass beneath our feet.

"Booby traps?" Sammy said. "Like poison darts and stuff?"

I remembered watching an old movie about an explorer who had to steal a golden idol, but before he could get to it, he had to walk across a stone floor. Some of the stones were booby traps and if he stepped on them, poison darts would shoot out of the walls. Goji must have been serious about keeping the Snarloks out if he'd gone to that trouble.

"Now what good would poison darts do against a gargoyle?" Gerty asked. "We're not trying to capture Indiana Jones after all."

WHOA! That was the guy I was thinking of! How'd she know his name? I suddenly imagined Gerty and my uncle watching old movies late at night, eating popcorn. I began to worry that we'd never find him.

"These are gargoyle traps," Gerty said. "And they're designed to keep gargoyles in, just as much as keep other things out. Snares, at a minimum. For the smaller ones, you understand." Then she chuckled. "There was this one time when Grimlo drank too much ale and stepped on a—" She stopped. "Oh, my, never mind. That wouldn't be polite at all." Her voice got serious again. "Suffice it to say that there are mechanical traps, as well as magical. I'm sure you can only imagine what it may take to restrain a gargoyle and the damage those traps would do to a normal boy or girl. Not to mention, some traps are not meant to only restrain. Which is why you'll follow my lead carefully until we pass the silver ring."

She turned and disappeared into the mist.

And we all followed, one by one.

THE GARGOYLE
REALM

One minute we were stumbling through the mist and tall grass, the next, we stepped onto the remnants of an ancient stone and gravel road, and the mist had thinned. The road seemed to have suddenly risen out of the field as if it had been buried there all along. The field still stretched out around us, but something was different in the air.

Gerty stood to the right of the stone road. It was about eight feet wide and looked like it had been built by the Romans.

"Walk carefully, dears," Gerty said. "Stay behind me and be mindful of where I step."

We walked in a zigzagging line, one after the other, behind Gerty. For a while I thought Gerty was smelling her way forward, but then realized she was looking very carefully at the stones.

We continued this way for a while, and I started to get bored. I wanted to see some gargoyles or something.

"Almost clear," she called back. "Straight away now."

After several more feet she stopped and looked back. "Now then—"

Gerty lunged for me as I stepped towards the middle of the path. Her mouth caught a beltloop of my pants, just as I stepped on a stone. As soon as my foot touched it, the middle of the road fell away in three large chunks. It was a booby trap!

With one foot on solid ground, my other foot (and leg and half my body) hung suspended over a giant void where the stones had just been. I looked down and saw nothing but space. It was deep black space with ancient stars. This gargoyle trap would have sent me falling out into space, but from the very ground we walked on.

Gerty gently pulled me back until I had my balance. We all stared in disbelief at the black void just inches beneath our feet.

"As I said, you'll follow me closely, until we pass the silver ring," Gerty said. She did not look pleased.

I nodded in agreement.

We resumed walking. After several minutes we came to another stone road. It crossed our path from right to left in a long slow curve and disappeared out of sight.

Stepping into the crossing of the two roads she stopped. "We made it."

"We did?" Suzy asked. "How can you tell?"

"We just crossed the silver line," Gerty said.

"Where?" I asked. "I don't see anything."

"That's because you're not looking in the right place," Gerty replied.

"Oh," Sammy said. "I think I see it. Hey guys, I think I see it!"

Sammy was looking behind us, where we'd just walked from. He was pointing to the ground.

"Yeah, I see it too," said Kat.

Then we all did.

A fine silver line, thin as a pencil lead and as faint as dust, ran along the outer edge of the curving road that crossed our path.

"It's so beautiful," Suzy said, "it could be made of starlight!"

"This is the outer ring," said Gerty. "From here, inward, there are no more booby traps. But—!" and she looked directly at me, "from here on, you are all to be on your best behavior."

Everyone else turned and looked at me, too.

JEESHH! Why does everyone look at me when things happen?

"Ok, ok," I said.

Gerty gave me a quick wink, then turned and continued walking.

The gargoyle realm wasn't like anything I'd ever seen before. The land stretched out in all directions and disappeared into the mist. It looked like the round top of Gargoyle Hill had been chopped off completely and replaced by another world.

As we walked, we saw large grassy fields between the intersecting stone roads. But they weren't overgrown or weedy like the hill was. The fields looked like grass courtyards, sectioned off by the stone paths. Within the courtyards sat stone platforms of all shapes and sizes: large squares of white granite, medium-sized circular platforms of black basalt, great round balls carved from blue rocks. There were even some pedestals carved from huge crystals, jutting out of the ground.

"What are those?" Sammy asked, pointing at the stone pedestals.

"Well, a gargoyle needs a place to crouch, doesn't it?" Gerty said.

Now it made sense. All those pedestals needed was a giant

statue, or gargoyle, standing on them to make them complete. Then it would almost look like a vast stone city, like New York: a city of monsters towering above us humans.

Somehow, the area of the gargoyle realm was much larger than my uncle's hill allotted for. I had to remind myself this was the Catskill Mountains, and that many things were not what they seemed.

Strange torches towered above the grassy courtyards, illuminating the stone platforms. Some areas had regular fire torches that burned a warm yellow at the top of tall wooden stakes. I could smell the wood smoke.

Other areas were lit by blue or green pulsing crystals perched atop thin metal poles. My skin tingled when we walked past them.

And some areas glowed blacksilver, lit by shimmering orbs suspended from spiderweb silk that hung from the heavens. I felt sleepy and dreamy all at the same time in this area.

And above it all, the oldest stars I'd ever seen twinkled in a deep black sky; ancient constellations marking gargoyle-time for all eternity.

"Wow," said Sammy, looking up, his double goggles perched on his face. "I can see trails in the air. Gargoyle paths I think."

"Perhaps," said Gerty.

"Where are all the gargoyles?" I asked, looking around.

"The gargoyle realm is enormous," Gerty said. "Some are already here, but most are still traveling. You'll see them soon enough."

Another crossroad emerged from the mist, just up ahead. It also ran from right to left. We were all looking around at the giant stone pedestals and strange lights when Kat called out, "Hey, look at that!"

That's when we saw the gnomes.

As if suddenly appearing like a magic trick, the crossroad, which had looked to be empty, was now bustling with activity. Gnomes were everywhere, moving in all directions, pushing, pulling, carrying, or rolling all manner of things.

"Wow!" said Sammy. "It's like a whole herd of them. Is that the right term, a herd of gnomes?"

We all shrugged. It sounded good to us.

"A 'catastrophe,' my dear," said Gerty.

"A what?"

"A large gathering of gnomes is called a 'catastrophe,'" said Gerty again. "You know, a pride of lions, a herd of elephants, a catastrophe of gnomes."

I scratched my head. "But why—?"

BANG!

SPROINGG!

CRASH!

KABBLAMO!

"Watch where yer goin', ya mutton head!" yelled a gnome.

"Outta my way, gobbleflot! This here cask is for Dargon!" said another gnome.

"BLANKITY, BLANK, BLANK!" said a third.

That was weird. He literally said, 'blankity, blank, blank.' Now I understood why they were called a *catastrophe*.

"Step lively," Gerty said. Then she was weaving her way through the gnomes.

We all ran after her trying not to get clobbered. The stone path shook like an earthquake. The gnomes here were just as heavy-footed as Grimlo. Sammy tripped over his shoelaces and would've gotten crunched if Kat hadn't saved him. She pulled him out of the way of a crazy-looking wagon with three gnomes riding in it.

WHOOSH! It zoomed right past us.

Gerty just missed getting her tail stepped on by a gnome who was balancing seven large crates on his head.

But Suzy managed the crossing easily. And was making new friends while she did it. Every other gnome that went by had to tip his hat at her.

"G'day missus," one said.

"Lovely vest, my lady," said another.

"Long days and pleasant nights," a third gnome offered.

"Hey, how ya' doin'?" said another. He sounded like he was from New Jersey. The last word stretched out into two long syllables, *dooo-innn.*

Then he got smacked by a stick.

"Keep your peepers to yourself!" said the gnome behind him. It was a girl gnome! It must have been his wife, but it was hard to tell. They all sort of looked the same.

"I was just bein' friendly," said the Jersey gnome, rubbing his head.

WHACK!

"Mr. Friendly, is it?" the girl gnome said. "I'll show you friendly!"

And away they went, bickering down the street.

Finally, we crossed the gnome road and made it onto a side path that continued forward. There was far less traffic here, just a few gnomes traveling to one of the inner circles.

"What are they all doing?" Suzy asked.

"They're preparing for the Dance, of course," said Gerty. "But don't worry about that now. We're to see Goji soon. But before we do, we'll have to cross Troll Bridge. Remember what I said about being on good behavior."

TROLL BRIDGE
(KAT AND SUZY)

As we walked, we began to smell something in the mist. It was mild at first but grew stronger the further we walked.

"Eww," Suzy said, holding her nose. "What's that smell?"

"Oh, man," Sammy replied, "it smells like dead fish."

"And rotten eggs," I said.

"That would be a moat," Gerty said.

"A moat?" Kat said. "Like the kind around a castle?"

"Sort of," Gerty replied. "But this moat doesn't surround a castle, it simply appears here as a test of our resolve. And in a way, it's a marker between the outer gargoyle realm and the inner."

"What do you mean, it 'appears here'?" I asked. "Like the moat has a choice?"

"Not quite, dear," said Gerty. "You see, when gargoyles come to palaver, they often project an image of their stones with them. And sometimes, a bit of the area around their stones."

"Oh, yeah," Sammy said. "I remember Grimlo saying something about 'where their stones lie' when he was talking about the gargoyles. It's like their home castle, or whatever they're stuck to. So, you're saying the moat will appear because it's close to some gargoyle stones?"

"I am," Gerty said.

"Oh, and the bridge goes over the moat," Sammy stated, nodding happily at his growing understanding.

"It does," Gerty confirmed.

"Hey, wait a minute." Sammy didn't look so happy now. "Does that mean there are gargoyles on the bridge?"

"It does, indeed," said Gerty, then stopped. "Behold, Troll Bridge."

In front of us, shrouded in mist, was an old stone bridge. Crumbling columns of stone stood at all four corners. A small gargoyle, which looked something like a flying monkey, sat atop each column. Burning torches hung from the columns, lighting the moss-covered stones of the bridge.

The bridge looked to only be six feet wide, not even as wide as the path we were on. From our side, the bridge rose in a gentle arch, then down to the other side of the moat. But it also arched from side to side. And it didn't have any rails! *Who builds a bridge like this?* I wondered. One wrong step and you could go sliding over the edge and into the stinking moat.

"Now remember, dears," Gerty said. "Best behaviors. Oh, and promise to think hard."

What did that mean?

And with that, she turned and walked onto the bridge, straight up the middle. Then she disappeared over the rise in the bridge and went out of sight.

"Uh, guys," Sammy whispered. "Wh-who wants to go first?"

Kat spoke up. "I'll go. I'm not afraid."

Kat walked forward. As soon as her foot touched the bridge, the gargoyle on the left opened its eyes and spoke.

"Who dares to cross this bridge of mine?"

Its voice was high and creaky, like an old witch's voice. If she were a flying monkey, that is.

Kat stopped so suddenly her feet almost slipped out from under her, and her arms flailed for balance. And she was barely on the bridge. I was afraid to think what would have happened if she had been at the slippery top.

"Uh, my name is Kat."

The gargoyle monkey continued. "Answer you must, to pay our toll. Or fail tonight and wake the troll."

"Wake the troll?" Sammy whispered. He began to squirm in his sneakers. "Oh man, not a troll."

He adjusted his double set of goggles and began scanning the mist for trolls.

"Relax," I whispered. "The troll is probably under the bridge. Besides, if you get all nervous, you're liable to slide right off into the moat with it."

Sammy's eyes went extra wide at the idea of meeting the troll beneath the bridge.

Then the gargoyle monkey spoke to Kat again. "How many months of the year have 28 days?"

Kat shrugged her shoulders and said, "That's easy, one."

"WRONG!" the gargoyle said.

The bridge shuddered once, dislodging a stone from the path. It fell into the water with a noisy SPLASH! Kat jumped back onto the hard ground for safety.

A few more of those and the bridge would fall apart, I thought. That is, unless all the noisy splashes woke the troll first.

"Wait," Suzy whispered to Kat. "It's a riddle, which means it's not an easy answer."

"I know what a riddle is," Kat said. "I just—" She stopped suddenly, realizing her mistake. "Darnit. The gargoyle didn't ask 'how many months have ONLY 28 days?' It asked, 'how many HAVE 28 days?' They all do! Duh."

"Yeah, that's right," Sammy said. "Try again."

Kat nodded, turned and stepped onto the bridge again. During our palaver the gargoyle had closed its eyes, but they sprung open again at the touch of Kat's foot.

"Who dares to cross this bridge of mine?"

"Kat."

"Answer you must, to pay our toll. Or fail tonight and wake the troll."

Kat nodded.

"How many months of the year have 28 days?"

"All of them," Kat said.

"You may pass," the gargoyle said. Then went back to sleep. Kat began a slow careful walk up the center of the bridge.

"Way to go!" Sammy yelled.

Suzy shushed him with her finger. "Shh... don't wake the

troll," she said. "It's my turn next."

Oh, sorry, Sammy mouthed, and motioned that he would be quiet.

Suzy walked up and stepped onto the bridge.

This time, the gargoyle monkey on the right opened its eyes.

"Who dares to cross this bridge of mine?"

It was the same, creaky witch-voice, but somehow the eyes looked a little different.

"Suzy."

"Answer you must, to pay our toll. Or fail tonight and wake the troll."

Suzy nodded.

"What has hands and a face, but can't hold anything or smile?"

Suzy turned and looked back at us. Quietly, she mouthed the word, *LAH*.

"What did she say?" I asked Sammy. "Is she saying 'lah'?"

Sammy shrugged. "It looked like it. What does 'lah' mean?"

Suzy waved her arms to get our attention. *LAH!* She mouthed, shaking her hands. *You know, LAH!* Then she began to flap her arms like a bird.

"Poor girl must be crazy with fright," Sammy said. "I think she's saying she needs help and wishes I could FLY over and save her." He said this with a kind of dreamy look on his face.

"Uh," I said, "I'm pretty sure she didn't say that."

Frustrated, Suzy shook her head and waved us off. She turned to the gargoyle and said, "Clock. The answer is a clock."

"You may pass," the gargoyle said, and went back to sleep.

"Oh…" Sammy whispered. "A clock." Only his words were exaggerated like, K-LAHH-CK. "That was my next guess, anyway."

"Yeah right," I said.

We watched as Suzy slowly made her way up the bridge. Then we turned and looked at each other.

Our turns were next.

TROLL BRIDGE (SAMMY AND MILO)

I motioned for Sammy to go next. For some reason, I thought it would be best for me to be last. Sammy walked towards the bridge and put one foot on the stone platform.

Nothing happened. The gargoyles remained asleep.

He turned, looked at me and shrugged, *What do I do now?*

I motioned for him to continue.

He took another step, then a third. Still, the gargoyles remained silent.

Sammy waved for me to come closer. I stepped up right to the edge of the bridge. "Maybe we can cross together," he whispered. "Let's try."

I shrugged. Why not? I thought. And took a step onto the bridge. Still nothing.

Awesome! I thought. This wouldn't be so hard after all.

Slowly, we walked up the incline of the bridge, careful of the slippery stones. The higher we got, the worse the smell became. I started to feel nauseous and light-headed. Ahead of me, Sammy wobbled a few times, and I wondered if the stench was having the same effect on him.

After what seemed like a long time (the bridge was longer than it looked), Sammy came to the apex of the bridge.

"Who dares to cross this bridge of mine?"

It was the gargoyle monkey at the end of the bridge that spoke this time, the one sitting on the lefthand column.

"Oh, no," Sammy croaked. "They stopped us at the top of the bridge."

"Just stand still," I said, "and let it ask its question."

"Ok," he whispered.

Then Sammy gave his name. "Uh… S—Sammy, uh, s—sir."

"What's wrong with you?" I whispered. "It's not a 'sir'!"

"Answer you must," the gargoyle began.

"H—how do you know?" Sammy whispered back. "I—I was just trying to be polite."

"—to pay our toll."

"Shhh!" I said.

"Or fail tonight—"

"Be quiet," he responded, "I can't hear."

"—and wake the troll."

Sammy shivered, whether from cold or nerves, but the gargoyle took it as a sign that he'd nodded in agreement.

"It belongs to you, but your friends use it. What is it?"

Sammy turned and looked at me. We were standing so close to

each other, we bumped our arms, and our feet slid.

Sammy's eyes were wide, searching for the answer to the riddle. Suddenly, we felt a wind began to blow and held each other's arms for balance. He gulped.

"I—I don't know," he whispered. "My goggles?"

"WRONG!" the gargoyle said, and the bridge shook again.

Two rocks fell off this time, both splashing noisily into the moat. Something groaned from below.

The troll! I mouthed silently and shook my head. *Don't wake it.*

Sammy clutched his head, as if trying to squeeze the answer free. I could see him mouthing, *oh man, oh man.*

Quietly I said, "Sammy, it must be something that you never use."

He replied, "Milo, why would I not use something if I owned it?"

"Sammy, it didn't say you owned it, just that it belongs to you." Then I added, "But your friends use it."

"What, like my—?" Sammy started, then stopped. His face lit up. "My name," he said. "My friends use my name, like you just did."

"You may pass," said the gargoyle.

Sammy gave me a thumbs up, grinning widely. Then turned and began a slow walk toward the other side.

I was the only one left.

I gulped and squinted into the mist. I could see outlines of Kat and Suzy standing on the other side, watching us. A gray lump lay on the ground in front of them. Was that Gerty? I wondered. Why was she laying down? Had she fallen asleep again? I thought she'd be more concerned about us crossing.

"Come on, Milo," Sammy whispered from down the bridge. "It's kind of shaky on this side. This is where the rocks fell out."

I gave him a thumbs up. Then stepped forward.

"Who dares to cross this bridge of mine?" the fourth gargoyle said. But this one stood up and stretched its stone wings.

"AH!" Sammy cried out when the gargoyle stood up. His feet slipped out from under him, and he hit the stones with a loud THUMP! Then I heard, "aaeeyyyy, oof, ow, ow," as he went sliding down the rest of the bridge. He bumped to a stop, then said, "Hey, I made it!"

I looked back at the gargoyle. It stared at me with white glowing eyes. Its wings began to flap slowly.

"Milo," I creaked.

"Answer you must, to pay our toll. Or fail tonight and feed the troll."

Hey, wait a minute! *Feed* the troll? That's not what the other gargoyle monkeys had said. What about *waking* the troll? Or making him really angry? I could deal with that. But *feed* the troll? Honestly, I'd rather clean the girl's bathroom, but I was pretty sure that wasn't a choice just now.

I nodded to the gargoyle.

"If you don't keep me, I'll break. What am I?"

Uh, oh, I thought. *I'm sunk.*

I stared at my friends on the other side of the bridge, wondering if this would be the last time I ever saw them. I mean, what kind of a riddle was that? I didn't even know where to begin.

I racked my brain trying to remember any riddles I'd heard

before. Nothing was coming to me. My head was full of knock-knock jokes.

I must have been taking too much time, because suddenly the gargoyle said, "Answer," and rose off the column.

YIKES!

It hovered above the stone column, flapping its creaky wings. Then all the gargoyle monkeys began to chant as one.

"Answer you must, to pay our toll. Or fail tonight and feed the troll.

"Answer you must, to pay our toll. Or fail tonight and feed the troll."

The bridge began to shake. Their chanting was shaking the stones loose. I heard several stones splash into the moat below. Then I heard something grumble again.

"ARRGGHHH-MMMM."

The troll was waking up.

I held my hands over my ears and closed my eyes. I had to concentrate. I thought about the riddle. *If you don't keep me, I'll break. What am I?*

The answer couldn't be as simple as a glass bowl or cup. That didn't make any sense. But anything could break, couldn't it? I'd even heard the older girls in my school say they had broken hearts before, but you couldn't keep a heart. Then I remembered what Gerty had said right before she crossed the bridge. 'Now remember dears, best behaviors. Oh, and promise to think hard.'

The bridge shook again as another stone fell away. My foot slipped and I started to slide to one side. The bridge was about to fall over. I clawed at the moss-covered stones, trying to hold on, but it seemed like the gargoyles wanted me to fall in.

Think, Milo! I said to myself. *Gerty said 'promise to think hard,' so you better—*

Hey, that was it! Something you should always keep.

"A promise!" I said to the gargoyles. "You should always keep a promise. If you don't, you break it."

And just like that, the gargoyles stopped chanting. The flying one settled back onto its column. The bridge stopped shaking.

"You may pass," the last gargoyle said. Then it closed its eyes.

"You did it!" Sammy yelled from the other side. He was pumping his fist in the air.

I walked carefully across the rest of the bridge. The troll grumbled once more from below, but fell silent. He'd gone back to sleep.

When I stepped off the bridge and back onto the stone road, my friends greeted me with high fives and fist bumps. My hands did their little happy dance again, scrunching together, then relaxing. Gerty was laying on the ground, curled up in a ball, sleeping. The noise of our celebration woke her.

"Ahh," she yawned and stood up, stretching the way dogs do. "Across already, dears?" She looked sleepily at each one of us. "Now then, that wasn't so bad, was it?"

"Wasn't so bad?" Sammy asked. "Oh man, the bridge almost fell down. One minute it was shaking, then the gargoyle flew up and the troll growled and—"

He stopped. His mouth hung open and all he could do was point. We all looked in the direction he was pointing. It was the bridge.

It was back to normal. I mean, there wasn't a stone out of place. The mist had stopped swirling and the stink of the moat was gone.

"You were saying, dear?" Gerty said. "Something about the bridge? Oh, the four monkey sisters, they are a mischievous bunch, aren't they? I hope they didn't give you much trouble."

"Much trouble?" I said. "That's an understatement. Gerty, why didn't they ask you a riddle when you crossed?"

"Me?" she replied. "Why, I've already answered my riddle. And once you've answered, you're free to cross whenever you like."

Whew! That was a relief, I thought. Then asked, "What riddle did they ask you?"

"What kind of dog never bites?" Gerty said.

We all looked at each other and shrugged.

"A hot dog, of course," she said and winked.

THE INNER REALM

Beyond the moat, as Gerty had stated, was the Inner Realm. It looked much different here.

In the Outer Realm, the grass courtyards had been spread wide with little crowding. Almost like a campground for gargoyles with few neighbors.

But crossing into the Inner Realm was like walking into an over-crowded city. If the grass courtyards were here, I couldn't see them. Every inch of ground was covered with stone platforms and pillars, stacked next to each other, awaiting their gargoyles. And many more gargoyles were already here.

As we walked, the paths became narrower, bringing the frozen stony faces closer to us. The paths had become alleys, winding their way through gargoyle walls. It was so tight, we had to walk single file. The stones were squeezing in around us, closer and closer. The air felt thick.

The streetlamps here were like the ones on my uncle's farm. They were tall and ornate, with old glass globes pointing towards the sky. But most of their light was blocked by gargoyle heads or stone arches or some other giant carving.

"Milo," Sammy whispered. I thought I heard his knees rattling. "Wha—What's that?"

I looked to where he was pointing. Up ahead of us the face of a dragon stuck out of a high wall. Its huge, bulging eyes looked down at us. Its face was twisted sideways into a snarl. Its tongue was so long, it came out of its mouth and curled up over its head. It looked like a whip.

I couldn't see Gerty, the stones were too close, but as soon as Suzy stepped under the gargoyle, it came to life.

"GGLLAAAHHGGG!" It roared, waggling its whip-tongue in the air, then snapping it against the ground with a sharp *CRACK!*

Suzy screamed and jumped back, knocking Kat backwards. Kat tripped and fell on her butt.

"Hey!" Kat cried.

"Sorry," said Suzy. She held her hand out to Kat to help her up. Kat eyed Suzy, then reluctantly took her hand, but sprung up under her own power.

"Thanks," Kat said quickly.

Suzy turned towards the gargoyle. "Why did you do that?" she asked.

"BLAAHHHH-LAA-LAA-LAA," The gargoyle said, as it bulged its eyes at her. Its sharp tongue swayed over its head like a cobra snake, waiting to strike.

Suzy turned to us and asked, "Now what do we do?"

Sammy typed furiously into his controller. I thought he was looking for an answer on his computer, but doubted he'd find anything there.

The gargoyle seemed to be annoyed by the typing sounds coming from the controller and turned its attention to Sammy.

Its eyes narrowed.

Sammy typed.

Its tongue swayed in the air.

Sammy typed.

The gargoyle waited.

Its tongue swayed.

Just as Sammy finished typing, he looked up and the gargoyle struck. Its long tongue snapped at Sammy, making a loud CRACK! right in front of his face.

"AHH!" Sammy yelled and jerked backwards, throwing his arms up. This sent him tumbling to the ground and his feet flew up in the air.

"Hey! Stop that!" I yelled, jumping in front of Sammy, Kat and Suzy. "All we want to do is pass!"

I stared the gargoyle straight in the face.

A rumbling began to vibrate through the stones. It felt like a very slow earthquake coming up from the ground. A few seconds later I realized it was the gargoyle. A slow, deep laugh emerged from its stone mouth. "Heh, heh, heh." Its voice shook the stones. "Little brave one." It stared right into my eyes.

Just then I thought I heard my own knees rattling and thought they were about to buckle. I remembered my mom telling me once that if I wanted people to respect me, I should look them in the eyes. I had no idea if this worked for gargoyles. But, what else could I do? I stiffened my knees. Then I stared right back.

The gargoyle said, "What brings you here, disturbing my sleep?"

I was totally improvising now. My mind flashed back to my uncle's den and the note I'd found there. One of the things on the training list said, *How to avoid offending a gargoyle.* So, I knew I had to be careful at this moment. Then I remembered Grimlo giving us a little bow when he'd presented us with our gifts in the front room. Maybe that would work, I thought.

"Begging your pardon… uh…" Just then, I realized I didn't know its name. I couldn't address it properly. "Umm, perhaps introductions are in order."

A look of surprise flashed over the gargoyle's face, then it was hidden away. I wondered if it thought I was mocking it. It looked at me for a long time. Finally, with the slightest nod of its head, it said, "I am Whipshot of the Wendigo clan. And I come to palaver."

I breathed a sigh of relief and thanked my lucky stars. This just might work out, I thought.

I raised my chin, then bowed my head ever so slightly and said, "I am Milo of the Savage clan. And I come to palaver."

Whipshot started to nod.

"With Goji," I finished.

Whipshot froze, his tongue snaking out of his mouth, tasting the air for an insult.

"I mean not to offend," I continued, "and would gladly palaver with you another time. But my quest is of an urgent matter and Goji would hear me forthwith."

Whipshot looked from one kid to the other, then back to me. Its tongue slid back inside its stone mouth. I was relieved to see it go. "Very well… Gargoyle Hunter."

In surprise, my hand shot to my chest. I felt for the talisman laying there beneath my shirt. How did he know? I wondered.

"I smelled it," Whipshot said. Then he nodded towards my chest. "The fragment of Moonstone you keep hidden."

I was no longer surprised that it seemed as if he'd read my mind. I was more interested in why he let me continue the conversation if he knew I had the Moonstone when I'd arrived.

"You could have announced your privilege," Whipshot said. "That you were a Gargoyle Hunter. And being one, you should be allowed to pass. But you chose not to exploit your privilege. And that shows compassion and restraint. I take no offense. Attend your business with Goji."

And just like that, Whipshot closed his eyes and let us pass.

THE GRAND COURTYARD

After passing Whipshot, the other members of the clan caught up to congratulate me, one by one.

"Well done," Suzy said. "Very clever to ask for introductions."

Then Kat stepped up and punched me in the arm. "Not bad, kid. At least you didn't blow it." Then she jumped up on some stone blocks and scrambled out ahead of us.

Finally, Sammy came up. "Hey Milo."

"Yeah?"

"Well… I just wanted to say thanks."

"For what?" I asked.

"Well… for kind of… sticking up for me. You know, when I tripped back there." He hesitated, then said, "You're a good friend." He slapped me on the shoulder, then let himself fall to the back of the line.

I thought about this weird group of kids that had been thrown into this crazy adventure. We'd formed a clan, but were we becoming more than that?

Yes. I thought we were.

Did I know anyone else who would volunteer to help me find an uncle they barely knew?

No. I didn't think so.

I suddenly realized that even though we were from different backgrounds, and everyone had different quirks (talents), that in the end, we might become good friends. If we let it happen.

We squeezed past a shimmering wall of gargoyle heads. They were stacked one on top of the other but looked like ghost faces. That was because they were still arriving, and their complete spirit wasn't here yet. In a way, this made them even creepier than Whipshot.

Sitting on the path in front of us was Gerty.

"Well, there you are, dears," Gerty said.

"Hey, where you'd go?" I asked.

"Oh, just visiting with some old friends."

"Old friends?" I said. "In here?"

"Well of course. It's been a year since I've visited. It's good to keep up relationships. You never know when you'll see someone again."

Man, wasn't that the truth, I thought. "But how did you know where to wait for us?"

"Oh, I had a hunch you'd come this way," Gerty said. "Besides, all roads lead to where you're going. Eventually." Then she winked at me.

What does that mean? I wondered. I was starting to feel like Gerty was the dog version of Yoda or something. But if I was supposed to be catching the hints… I sure wasn't getting them.

After passing several more gargoyle stones that were half here and half not, we passed through the inner realm and stopped. We'd just made it to the edge of the Grand Courtyard.

The Grand Courtyard looked similar to the outer realm, but it was a large circle. And it was dedicated for one gargoyle only: Goji the High Justice.

A path of crystals created the border around the courtyard. Inside the path of crystals was a circular strip of grass. Inside the strip of grass was a final circle of crystals. In the middle of the crystal circle sat Goji's white marble platform. A throne.

I couldn't see any streetlamps here, but it was very bright. The light seemed to radiate out of the crystal paths and the granite platform glowed.

I hadn't realized it until we were standing before Goji's throne, but ever since meeting up with Gerty, I had been leading us. Somehow, my wandering feet just knew where to go.

Suddenly, a column of mist came down from the sky and landed on the glowing platform. Tendrils of mist moved inside of it.

We walked forward, into the grand courtyard, and waited.

Goji was coming.

GOJI

Here, all was quiet. The hustle and bustle of the gnomes was far behind us. The stink of the moat was gone. The snapping tongue of Whipshot was still. Even the stars seemed to be more at ease here. Only a faint humming sound, like high-voltage electric lines, could be heard. The sound was coming from the column of mist that floated down onto the white marble platform.

We stood in silence, waiting.

The sky above us was black, the deepest space I'd ever seen. The stars looked down at us from their faraway places. I felt very small just then, tiny and insignificant, and wondered if I was up to the task of saving my uncle. Despite the recent successes, I was afraid that maybe I'd still fall short.

Just then the column of mist brightened. It had been gray like the clouds, but began to turn blue. Blue like a summer sky, then like the ocean. As the color changed, the electric humming grew louder.

The column of mist began to vibrate like a living thing. The light changed again, going from blue to bright white. We had to shield our eyes with our hands. We couldn't look at it; it was like staring into a white-hot sun that was settling to earth.

When the light dimmed, and we could see again, the column of mist had sunk to the ground. It spread out around our feet in waves, an ocean of mist.

Goji stood before us on the white marble platform.

Actually, he crouched. He was a gargoyle after all.

He stood on four strong legs that ended in great claws. His thick neck held a large head crowned with horns. Large stone teeth lined his mouth. Finely carved stone bat wings were folded across his back. A long thin tail curved out behind him, studded with spikey horns. His eyes were like green emeralds.

Gerty bowed, then looked at each of us. We bowed to Goji.

Goji bowed his head slightly and said, *Greetings,* although he didn't speak with his mouth. His voice came into our heads like a low rumble. It wasn't unpleasant, like hearing Whipshot laugh, but it pulsed with power. I imagined that if he was angry and spoke loudly, it might split my head wide open.

Then he spoke again.

Palaver we must, on the full moon.

The world is in need, this summer of June.

The secret is kept by not one alone,

Protect it you must, the all-sacred stone.

His green dragon eyes looked at each one of us as he said this. Once again, he only spoke inside our minds, but we all knew that each person had heard the same thing. It was as if I could hear Goji's words echoing into the minds of Sammy, Suzy and Kat. Somehow, I even knew that Gerty had heard him.

But what did he mean? It sounded similar to the chant I'd heard the first night on the hill. But that time there were multiple voices, chanting together. Was it another riddle, I wondered?

Goji looked at me as soon as I thought *riddle*. He seemed to be seeing inside my head, reading my thoughts, measuring my ability to understand his words.

I knew that the gargoyles needed to palaver, and I knew it had to happen during the full moon.

The secret is kept by not one alone. What did that mean?

Then I remembered: the museum! The stone warrior had said, 'The secret has been found.' But he never told me what the secret was. He must have been talking about the secret of how the Moonstone works.

Someone other than my Uncle Horace knows the secret of the Moonstone.

That's what the stone warrior was trying to tell me. Which is why the Snarlok attacked him. And that's what Goji was telling me now.

Goji's green eyes glittered when I thought this. My friends all looked at me. "I think you're right," said Sammy. "Someone else knows the secret."

WHOA! Now everyone can read my mind. That was a scary thought.

"No," said Gerty. "We can't read your mind, Milo. We can only hear each other's thoughts when we're connected to Goji. He hears our thoughts and sends them out to the group."

Goji spoke again.

Find the one, who stands alone
In the golden rays, on morning's stone.

147

A question she'll ask, and answer you must,
Look deep within, to those whom you trust.

I scratched my head and looked at my friends. Sammy's goggle-eyes blinked back at me. Suzy was writing something in her book. Kat stood with her hands on her hips, waiting for me to say something.

So I said, "What?"

"Well?" Kat tapped her foot on the ground. "What's the plan?"

"Uh… the plan?" I asked.

"Yeah, you know, like first we'll do this, then we'll do something else. You know, a plan."

"Well…" I said.

"You do have a plan, don't you?" Kat squinted her eyes at me.

"Yes," I said quietly.

Her eyes narrowed further to squinty slits. "Then what is it?"

"Come on, Milo," Sammy interrupted. "Tell 'em your plan."

I looked at Sammy in surprise. What was he doing?

"Yeah," Sammy continued, "Milo's got a plan. Just like when he got us past Whipshot. Isn't that right? Yeah, Milo's got lots of plans. In fact, he's the *MAN* with the *PLAN*!" Then he punched me in the arm as if to say, 'Well, that's that.'

I gulped, then said, "Er… well… the plan is to… solve the riddle."

"Of course!" Sammy said. "The riddle. That's an awesome plan! The only reason Goji gave us the next riddle was because Milo solved the first one so quickly. Isn't that right, Milo?"

He smiled at me with both thumbs in the air.

WE FIND
A STAR MAP

My stomach felt kind of queasy, and I began to sweat. I hadn't really solved Goji's riddle; I sort of guessed at it. I mean, if the stone warrior hadn't warned me, I don't think I would have figured it out at all.

I really missed my mom just then. I wondered if I'd ever see her again, or if she was even alive. I swallowed hard and put on my best face. It was nerve wracking having so many people looking to me for answers. That normally didn't happen to me.

I looked up into the night sky wondering what to do. I had to figure out a way to solve Goji's riddle.

As I stared at the sky, my imagination took over. I had always imagined seeing shapes in clouds. Sometimes I saw things form in the combination of leaves on trees. The same thing was happening now. I was seeing shapes in the stars.

At first, I thought it was just my imagination, but the longer I looked, the more my brain was certain something was there. But I couldn't figure out what I was seeing.

I leaned my head way back and looked at the stars straight overhead. Then I looked up to my left, then over to my right.

"What is it?" Kat asked, looking up.

"What do you see?" said Suzy. She craned her head back.

"Oh man," said Sammy, fidgeting with his goggles. "I can't see a thing. I think the batteries are low."

I was seeing letters form in the night sky. Far away, the stars seemed to be aligning as letters laid out in a large circle. As I walked around, looking left and right, I realized the star-letters were centered high above Goji's platform. They seemed to go around in a circle, just like the gargoyle realm.

"Hey guys, look at that," I said. "Do you see it?"

Everyone looked up.

"What?"

"Where?"

"What do you see?"

I pointed straight up. "There, doesn't that look like the letter V? And over there, the letter I. A bunch of them. In a circle."

"I don't see—" Kat started, "hey wait a minute. I do see!"

"Yeah," said Suzy. "And there's an X!"

"Where?" I asked. "I don't see an X."

"Over there." She pointed. "Hey, that's strange," Suzy said. "That looks like a clock."

"Oh, man," Sammy said, still fiddling with his goggles. "I want to see too!"

"A clock?" I asked.

Suzy was now walking around the stone platform with me. "Yes.

Those letters are roman numerals. They're laid out in a circle. It's a clock. Actually, it's a star-clock."

"Got it!" Sammy said. Then he was staring up into the night sky with the rest of us.

"You're right!" I said. "It is a star-clock. But why would there be a star-clock out here? What does it mean?"

"Uh, guys," Sammy said. "You gotta see this." He took his goggles off and handed them around.

We all took turns looking through Sammy's goggles. It took a while to adjust the straps for each person's head, but in the end, we all saw the same thing.

As we looked at the star-clock, we saw the roman numerals representing each number, one through twelve. But we also saw five blinking lights, clustered together near the center of the clock. Those lights were us. Somehow, the goggles that Grimlo had given Sammy could see us represented on the star-clock.

I took the goggles one last time. "It's not just a star-clock," I said. "I think it's also a star-map." I handed the goggles back to Sammy.

"You're right," said Sammy. "With the goggles I can see our trail. Or what's left of it. It sort of looks like stardust, or how the Milky Way looks, but thinner. It seems to be fading, but if that is a map, I'm pretty sure we came into the realm by the number six."

"By the six?" I asked.

"Yeah," said Sammy. "Like if we'd walked onto a big clock. When we crossed the creek on your uncle's farm and climbed Gargoyle

Hill, according to this, we came in around the number six, at the bottom of the star-clock. Now we're standing in the center, where the clock hands connect."

"I was watching my compass," Suzy said. "We mostly walked North to get here. Although… I'm not sure if compasses work the same here."

I had an idea.

"But if they do," I said, "then I think we have to go to the number three."

"What? Why do you say that?" Kat asked.

Suzy checked her notepad, then read. "Find the one, that stands alone. In the golden rays, on morning's stone."

"It's another riddle," I said. "Grimlo told us my uncle was also the guardian of the Midday Gate, right?"

Everyone nodded.

"And we walked into the Gargoyle realm through the Midday Gate, which is by the number six on the star-clock."

Everyone nodded again.

"And now we have to find someone who stands on the morning's stone, in golden rays, you know, like 'in the morning.' And where do golden morning rays come from?"

Now everyone just stared at me.

"From the east!" I said. "And East on our star-clock-map would be at the number three."

Sammy just blinked at me.

Suzy consulted her notes.

Kat scratched her chin and stared at me.

"Isn't that right?" I turned to ask Goji, but the platform was bare. Goji was gone.

"You know," Suzy finally said, "you might be onto something. It sounds crazy. But you just may be right."

"Uh, guys?" Sammy said, looking up at the star-map. "I think something is following us."

A NEW DIRECTION

"Following us?" Suzy said. "What's following us?"

"I'm not sure," said Sammy. "But I see other trails in the sky. Now that I know what I'm looking for, I see a lot of stuff."

"Like what?" Kat asked.

Sammy adjusted his goggles again. "They look like shooting stars, only I think they're going around in a circle. Around the star-clock. They must be really far away, because they haven't moved very far since I've been watching them. But they *are* moving."

"Moving where?" Suzy asked.

"Around in a circle, I think, sort of like the second hand is shooting stars and they're flying around the star-clock. There are blue ones, and purple ones, but they're moving at different speeds. There's a bunch of them."

"Different colors running at different speeds?" Kat said. "Maybe time runs at different speeds for gargoyles. Maybe the star-clock keeps track of all the different times, for all the gargoyle clans, across the world."

"Actually," I said. "That's not a bad idea."

"What do you mean, *actually*?" Kat said, glaring at me. "Like boys are the only ones who can have good ideas? Huh? I don't think so."

"Sor-ryy," I said, shrugging. "I was just—"

"Uh, guys," Sammy interrupted. "About the things..."

"What things?" I asked.

"The things following us," Sammy said.

"Oh, yeah."

"And why do you think they're following us?" Suzy asked.

Sammy lifted his goggles and stared at us. "Because one of the shooting stars is no longer traveling in a circle. When it got close to the number four it broke off its path. It's heading for the center."

"The center? Where we're standing now?" Suzy asked.

"Yeah, I think so," said Sammy. His feet started tapping. "Oh man, oh man. And there's one more thing. All the other shooting stars are blue, purple or silver. The one heading towards us is red."

"Red?" said Kat. "Like the red tentacles of the Snarloks?"

"I don't know. Maybe," said Sammy.

"Come along, dears," Gerty said. "Our time is growing short."

We followed Gerty around the magnificent stone pillar, then turned to the right. The path we'd walked in on, the one that crossed Troll Bridge and wound through the inner realm, now trailed off into the mist, also to our right. The Midday Gate was somewhere far back there. Ahead of us was...

"Easterling," Gerty said. "It's been a long time since I've been to Easterling."

"What's Easterling?" Sammy asked. His giant eyeballs blinked through his goggles.

Gerty continued walking and spoke to us without looking back. "Milo's Uncle Horace has explored further than any other Gargoyle Hunter I know of. He's mapped much of the southern and eastern parts of the gargoyle realm. The southern part is called Midday, as you might have guessed. That's where we came in.

"And Milo is correct, Easterling is in the direction of the number three; if you're looking at the star-clock, that is. There are entrances to the realm at both locations. One of them, as you know, is at Milo's uncle's farm, on Gargoyle Hill. A second gate is in Easterling. I suspect that is where we'll find the morning stone."

"What about the other directions?" Suzy asked. "Are there gates in the west and north?"

"There are rumors of a gate in Westworld," Gerty said. "But I don't believe anyone knows where it is. It's rumored to move from place to place, as if floating on the shifting sand. One story even places the west gate underground, in an abandoned mine, in a deserted town called Desperation. And in that version of the story, the gate is guarded by an evil spirit."

Sammy shuddered. "Eeww, evil spirits."

"Wicked," said Kat.

"But what about north?" asked Suzy. "There must be something in the north, isn't there?"

Gerty stopped and turned towards us. I'd never known a dog to have a serious looking face before, but that's exactly what I saw.

"Midnight Land," Gerty said. "Where things walk backwards, and time is undone. If there is a gate there, I know of no one who has seen it."

We all stared at each other. Kat didn't even say anything. Midnight Land sounded like a place we didn't want to visit.

We walked on like this for a while.

At some point Sammy stopped fidgeting with his goggles and came up to my side. "Hey, Milo," he whispered. "I've been meaning to ask. What's that thing you do with your hands when you get excited?"

I self-consciously shoved my hands into my pockets. "What do you mean?" I said.

"Oh, I didn't mean anything by it," Sammy said. "I was just wondering... well, I mean I don't care if your fingers go crazy sometimes. My toes do the same thing when I get nervous. I've just never met another kid whose body did weird things like mine. But we can be friends anyway, right?"

"Of course we can," I said, relieved. "After all, we're a clan, right?"

Sammy smiled. "You betcha!"

"Oh, and before I forget," I said. "Thanks for sticking up for me back there with the whole 'plan' thing."

"No problemo," Sammy said and slapped me on the arm.

My hands did their little happy dance again, but I barely noticed.

"Time check, please," said Gerty.

Suzy looked at her watch. "Hey, wait a minute," she said. She tapped the face of her watch with her finger, then held it to her ear, listening to it. "This can't be right. It says it's almost seven o'clock already."

"So?" I said.

"So? Remember my alarm?" Suzy said. "We have to turn around

at 7:25. That'll be the three-hour mark. We must have time to get back."

"That's right," said Sammy. "If we don't make it back onto the porch by 11:59, something bad might happen. Grimlo said so."

"Uh, Sammy?" Kat said. "Don't forget that something bad may happen before then."

"What do you mean?" Sammy asked.

"Can I see your goggles?"

Sammy handed the special goggles to Kat, then pushed his other pair on top of his head and rubbed his eyes.

Kat held the goggles to her face and scanned the star-clock. "Oh, no," she whispered. Tossing the goggles back to Sammy, Kat said, "Look."

Sammy quickly scanned the sky. "Oh man! Oh man!"

"What?" I asked.

Sammy danced from foot to foot as he pointed at the night sky. "The things... the go-arounds... the chasers..."

"The what?"

He looked at us with large blinking eyes. "The red things in the sky! The things following us. They're getting closer!"

Just then I felt a tingle in the air. It was dark and I couldn't see anything, but the air had a tingly feel. It felt like static electricity that makes your hair stand up.

Something was moving in the air. Something large. It seemed to come from behind us, but it was getting closer. I could feel it moving the mist.

"Milo, your necklace," Kat said.

I looked down at the stone that hung around my neck. It was glowing.

"The Snarloks?" I asked.

"Oh man," Sammy said, dancing back and forth on his feet. "Not the Snarloks!" He spun in all directions, trying to spot them.

"Come now," Gerty said. "Quickly! Single file. We've tarried too long."

We all began to run.

THE CHASE BEGINS

We ran from the grand courtyard, heading east. As we passed outside the last crystal path, the narrow gargoyle alleys returned. We squeezed between the bulging stones. Gargoyle heads jutted out from ghost walls, leering at us in the darkness.

The gargoyles were not happy to be disturbed.

Gerty led us, followed by Suzy, Kat, Sammy, then me. Left and right we turned. Sometimes the gargoyle faces were surprised to see us, sometimes they were mad. A few times, a gargoyle would wake up in surprise, open its mouth as if it were going to scream, then blow its tongue at us.

PPLLLLGGHHTTT!!

Gargoyle spit covered my face.

Oh, gross! Talk about stinky! But I shouldn't have been surprised. After all, gargoyles don't have to brush their teeth for hundreds of years.

Strange images slid past us as we ran. The columns of mist were back, transporting more gargoyle spirits into the realm. Sometimes the mist slid along the ground like a snake, then suddenly shot into the air to form a shape. Sometimes fat columns of mist sunk down out of the night sky, hovering over a stone base. Gargoyle faces continued to appear out of the mist, an eye, a fang, part of a wing, or sometimes just the clawed feet.

We passed out of the inner realm. There was no moat here to divide the inner realm from the outer. But the stone paths widened and meandered through the grassy courtyards, just like before.

Gerty mostly ran in a straight line, but occasionally jumped from side to side. We were careful to do the same.

The grass courtyards here were like the ones we'd seen in Midday. Each had a stone pillar in the center and was illuminated by its own unique lamp or torch. But most of the lamps here looked like they'd been made in an old blacksmith's forge. The lamps were tall, with metal arms curving out in ornate designs. They reminded me of scenes from creepy old movies set in England. The lamplight, shining through these curves, cast strange shadows on the ground that looked like writing. I imagined that the shadows were gargoyle spells of some kind.

Just then I felt a rumble through my sneakers. The ground had begun to shake and the air vibrated. Wave after wave of mist blew past our heads, as if some giant thing was panting, right behind us. I turned and looked over my shoulder. The mist was rushing towards us in faster and faster waves. Something was chasing us, and it was close.

Just then, Sammy tripped on a loose cobblestone and went sprawling onto the ground in front of me. I was still looking backwards when this happened and tripped over Sammy's leg and

CRASH!

OOMPHH!

fell on top of Sammy.

"Ow!" yelled Sammy. Then, "My goggles!"

We rolled to a stop in the middle of the stone path. The giant thing in the mist was right behind us.

"Sorry!" I yelled. "Quick, get up. We have to get out of here!"

"My ankle," said Sammy. "I twisted my ankle on that rock."

"Come on, come on!" I screamed and pulled at his arms.

"The goggles!" he yelled. "Don't forget the goggles!"

I searched around on the misty path as Sammy struggled to his feet. He got up and began limping around the path. "Oh, man," he said, "it hurts really bad."

"I found them!" I said. "Come on, quick!"

Sammy put one arm over my shoulder, and we ran, limping, along the path. We'd lost sight of Gerty and the others. We were all alone.

Up ahead I saw another stone path crossing the one we were on. I thought if we could just make it there, we might be safe.

"Ow! I can't make it!" said Sammy. "My ankle!"

"Come on, Sammy," I said. "We have to try. Just a little further."

Just then something snagged my own ankle, and we tumbled to the ground again. I turned and looked.

A red ghost tentacle had grabbed me.

"Run, Sammy!" I yelled. "Run and find Gerty!"

I kicked at the ghost tentacle as my talisman glowed bright red beneath my shirt. It was a Snarlok warning sign. Waves of red light pulsed from it as the ghost tentacle gripped my ankle tighter. This tentacle was smaller than the ones that had attacked me and Mom at the house, but it was still strong.

I felt around for a loose stone to clobber the thing with. I still couldn't see a face, but a second slender tentacle snaked out of the mist.

I kicked my legs wildly, trying to keep it from getting a hold on my other leg. If that happened, it would probably pull me straight into the mist, I thought. The tentacles had small suckers on them, but they were sticky like suction cups. One of them stuck to the bottom of my sneaker and

POP!

off it came.

"Hey!" I yelled and grabbed my sneaker back. "That's mine!" I started hitting the small, soft end of the tentacle with my shoe.

"Eeeeeee!" it hissed. It didn't like that very much.

"Take that, you sneaker-stealing-Snarlok!" And hit it over and over again.

"Eeeeeee!" it hissed again.

Suddenly my leg was jerked hard, and I was pulled several feet into the mist. My head hit the hard ground and my sneaker flew out of my hand. I saw stars swirling around my head, but not the kind in the sky, the kind you get when you bang your head on something. I was jerked again, and my vision dimmed. I was about to pass out.

"Hey, Snarlok!" I heard Kat say, from somewhere behind me. "Let go of my friend!"

Then I heard an arrow whiz through the mist. It struck the tentacle holding my leg and the Snarlok screamed in pain.

"EEEEEEE!!!"

The tentacle released me, then flailed wildly in the air. It smashed down onto the cobblestone path. Again and again, it smashed the ground right next to me, trying to impale me with the arrow that stuck out of its tentacle.

I scrambled backwards and felt Sammy pulling me to my feet. "You dropped this," he said, and handed back my sneaker.

The ghost tentacle flailed twice more, then slid back into the mist.

Sammy and I turned around and saw an awesome sight. The whole group had come back for us. Gerty was panting but sniffing the mist for other Snarloks. Suzy was checking her watch to see how much time we had left. And Kat was still crouched on top of the rock from where she'd shot the Snarlok. Her bow and arrow still drawn, as she watched the mist behind us.

Yeah, she was definitely a ninja.

A CRAZY BOAT

"Wow, that was awesome," I said to Kat when we got back on our path. We were heading east again. "Where'd you learn to shoot like that?"

"The Boy Scouts," Kat replied.

"The Boy Scouts?" Sammy said. His goggles were back on, and his giant eyes blinked in surprise. "Like, with real boys?"

"Yeah, with real boys!" Kat said. "You think I can't compete against boys?" Kat turned around and stared at Sammy, her hands defiantly on her hips.

"You'd better watch it," I whispered to Sammy.

"I… I know," he whispered back. "I d-don't want to get clobbered or anything."

"Come along, dears," Gerty said. "Enough teasing. We have a bit further to go and need to stay together." Then she looked at Suzy. "Time check please."

Suzy had been reading the book that Grimlo had given her and checking her watch the last several minutes. She looked worried.

"I just can't figure this out," Suzy said. "It doesn't make sense."

"What doesn't make sense?" I asked.

"According to my watch," said Suzy, "only a few minutes have passed since our last time check. But that can't be right. We walked a long way before realizing Sammy and Milo were missing, then had to backtrack to find you guys. Then it took time to walk back to where we are now."

"What time is it?" Gerty asked.

"It's only 7:05," said Suzy. "It's only been about ten minutes since the last time you asked. How is that possible?"

"Oh, a lot of things are possible here," Gerty said. Then she stopped.

We had just arrived at the next path that ran through the outer realm, only, it wasn't a path. It was a river!

Well, it was probably more like a canal, like in Venice, Italy. We all stood at the edge of what should have been another stone path. We could see the path running from left to right in a sweeping arc, but it was covered with clear running water. The water was so clear we couldn't tell how deep it was, maybe only a few inches or maybe several feet. But it was deep enough to support boats. And boy were there a lot of boats!

It was just like when we'd come in at Midday Gate and saw all the gnomes hauling cargo on wooden carts, or carrying them on their heads. The gnomes were still hard at work, only here they moved everything on wooden boats.

Boats, canoes, and rafts of all sizes floated along the canal. Some of them had sails, some of them were guided by long poles, and some of them just bobbed along. But all of them were manned by cement garden gnomes.

"Aarrr... look out ya swarthy dog!" yelled one gnome. "Yer paddlin' the wrong way!"

WHOA! That one sounded just like Grimlo!

"Aarrr, you dim?" the other gnome yelled back to the first. "I be haulin' yesterday's loot. I have to paddle backy-wards!"

"Ahoy then," the first gnome said, "fair weather to thee."

Oh man! They all sounded like Grimlo! He must be from Easterling, I thought. No wonder he sounded like a pirate. They all had to use boats here.

We watched as the boats and rafts sailed back and forth, side to side, barely missing each other. I expected to hear a giant crash at any second, but each gnome guided their craft deftly between the others. Somehow the whole thing worked.

"Oh man," Sammy said. "How are we ever going to get across that?"

"Not to worry, dears," Gerty said. "Our transport is arriving now."

For the first time we noticed a small wooden dock upstream to our left. Some boats had stopped there briefly during the time we'd been standing here, but we had ignored them. Now, the craziest thing we'd ever seen had just bumped to a stop against the dock. We all followed Gerty as she walked out onto the wooden dock.

Before us, bobbing in the clear water, was a large wooden crate, just a box really. On top of the crate, connected with old ropes and fishing nets, was another layer of wooden boxes (crates), and above that, another layer made with more boxes and ropes. The whole contraption looked like a crazy invention from a Dr. Seuss book.

It reminded me of an upside-down pyramid that might have been made by the Whos down in Whoville. I couldn't figure how it didn't tip over.

"Climb aboard, dears," Gerty said.

And we all stared at Gerty with our mouths hanging open.

"Uh..." I said.

"Uh..." said Sammy.

"Well..." Suzy said, scratching her head.

"Awesome!" Kat said, and scrambled up the side, hanging from the ropes like a monkey.

There was a small catwalk of boards that ran around the perimeter of the lowest crate. It was like a skinny wooden sidewalk that sat just above the water line. Gerty jumped onto the catwalk, then turned around and looked at us. "Next?" she said. "Time is short."

"Theoretically," Suzy said, "wooden craft can be quite stable. Early explorers traveled long distances on boats smaller than this."

"Yeah, but they weren't made of used shipping crates," I said.

"True."

"AALLLL ABOARRDDD!" a voice boomed from the very top of the floating contraption.

I looked up and saw a gnarled gnome-face staring back at me. "This here vessel is departing, in 3... 2..."

We all scrambled on board! I jumped on and grabbed a rope. Suzy climbed up past me and followed the catwalk to where Gerty was. Sammy had just reached out when the captain said

"...1! Hare we go!"

Sammy leaped just in time. I caught his hand as the wooden contraption bumped, shuddered, then leapt away from the dock. The top of the 'boat' leaned over precariously. Sammy barely had time to grab a rope with one hand as I grabbed his other. As the boat sailed away from the dock, his legs flew out over the water. He looked like he was flying for just a minute. Then the boat tipped the other way, and he was flung up into a nest of ropes, where he was caught, hanging upside down.

"Are you OK?" I asked. "You almost didn't make it!"

His oversized eyes blinked wildly, upside down, as he patted himself down, looking for injuries. "I… I think I'll stay right here for a few minutes," Sammy said.

"Upside down?" I asked.

"Oh, it's really not that bad," he said. "Not bad at all."

"Suit yourself," I said, and started climbing for the top.

A HARROWING RIDE

At the top of the stack of crates was a flat area made of boards. They were strapped together with what looked like thin twine, the kind you might see holding a hay bale together. Around the edge of the platform was a rickety railing made of old tree limbs, mismatched stair spindles, and curved pieces of wood that looked like they'd come from wine barrels. In the center of the platform sat another wooden crate about two-feet square. And on top of the crate stood a garden gnome.

"Hammerling at yer surface!" the gnome said, bowing.

I knew he meant to say, 'at your service,' but wasn't sure if that's how he pronounced the word or had just made a mistake.

"Hammerling?" called Gerty from below. "Straight away, now. Uncle Horace is in trouble!"

"Aye, my lady! Ol' Hammerling is at yer surface, I am!" And with that he began to pull on the many ropes that were strung about.

What I thought were a nest of ropes holding the railings to the boxes, and the higher boxes to the lower ones, turned out to be the contraption's steering mechanism. As Hammerling pulled and yanked on the tangle of ropes, the crazy boat pitched this way and that, rocking from side to side.

I had to grab the railing to keep from falling overboard.

Kat whooped and hollered as her feet flew into the air. It was as if she were on the best rollercoaster in the world.

I heard Sammy moan from somewhere below. "Ohhh... I'm gonna be sick..."

"Ahoy there, mates!" Hammerling yelled. "Stow the stowy thing and jib the jabbermast!

"Aye, Aye, Captain!" Hammerling said to himself, then sprung off the box.

BOINGG!

He jumped off his captain's perch and went bouncing around the edge of the platform, pulling more ropes and yanking on boards. Apparently, he was the captain, first mate, second mate, and cabin boy, all rolled into one. At least, he thought he was.

"Ow! Oof!" Sammy said from below. "Who's pulling the ropes?"

The top-heavy boat teetered one way, then tottered another. Suddenly we were careening across the canal, swerving in between boats and rafts, barely missing them by inches. And we were sailing *upstream*, apparently without a sail or motor.

WEIRD!

"Aye captain," Hammerling yelled to himself. "The jibs are jabbed but we're taking on water fast. I think we be sinkin'!"

SPROING! BAM!

Hammerling landed back on the captain's perch with a loud

thud. "Aarrr, you dim, matey?" he said to himself. "That there is the bunghole ballast valve. It'll settle itself momentarily."

I'd heard of ballast tanks before, which were special tanks in ships that could store water. They helped stabilize the ship when it sailed. And sure enough, within a few minutes the ship stopped rocking and suddenly we were smooth sailing.

"Excellent work," Gerty said from below. "Now, straight on to the Easterling gate, if you please."

"Aye, my lady," Hammerling said. "The Easterling gate it is!"

Several minutes later, I heard grunts and groans coming from below. Then, Gerty's head popped up from the side. She'd climbed up a rope ladder that had been knitted into the tangle of ropes. Next came Suzy, then came a very green looking Sammy.

"Uugghhhh…." Sammy moaned. "Are we there yet?"

"Come now," Gerty said. "Stand up and clear your head. You'll miss the best part."

We all walked to the front of the platform and gazed out. From our position, and peering east, the realm looked like a magical painting. The chaotic canal we'd been on just a few minutes ago had led us to a serene lake that stretched out to the horizon. All the other boats and rafts were gone. We were the only ones out here.

This was quite a surprise to us, because when we'd been on the other side, the canal hadn't looked that wide. But now, and from this height, all we could see was water. Despite the late hour—it was after seven o'clock after all—the water before us sparkled as if from a bright morning sun. Rays of sunlight shot up from the surface of the water, splintering into every color of the rainbow. We had to shield our eyes from the bright light.

The shores of the lake were far away, and beyond them, the landscape looked like a watercolor painting. The shapes were wavy and mysterious, only hinting at what they might be.

We sailed like this for a while, almost as if in a dream. The light was magical and seemed to pull us forward. My eyes felt heavy, as if they wanted to sleep. We all stood, gazing into the magical light, dreaming wonderful things.

After a while, the light changed again, and the heaviness wore off. My eyes popped open, and I realized at some point we had entered another canal. We were now sailing along a straight canal—due east—that connected to the lake.

"What just happened?" asked Sammy. "Did I fall asleep?"

"I think I did," said Suzy. "And had a wonderful dream."

As we shook off the dreamy feeling of the magical light, we noticed that we were no longer towering above the water. It looked as if we were floating right on its surface. Somehow the stack of crates and boxes had shrunk down to a very small size. Or, the landscape had gotten taller.

This canal was bordered on each side by low walls made of stone. The water lapped right up to the top edge of the stones in gentle waves. Wide sidewalks of cobblestones ran along each side of the canal. But there was nothing beyond the sidewalks. Just like the watercolor look of the far-away shores, the air beyond the sidewalks was wavy and dreamy. Nothing had a solid shape, and I wondered if we weren't still dreaming.

Tall, ornate lamp posts jutted up from the sidewalks, lighting our way forward. The ancient lamp posts—and their strange crystal globes—cast magical, rainbow light in all directions.

"We're getting close now," said Gerty. "Come along dears, down to the catwalk."

And just like that, Gerty climbed down the rope ladder and waited.

The rest of us climbed down, Sammy very slowly, Kat swung on a rope. We waited to dock.

With the lightest touch, Hammerling brought the crazy boat to a stop, right at the edge of a stone dock.

Then his head looked over the side of the high platform. "Fare thee well, my lady," Hammerling said quietly. "And may ye' find Horace before the vurry bad thing happens." With that, he saluted her and disappeared out of sight.

"Thank you, Hammerling," Gerty said. Then, "Come along, dears. Time waits for no one."

I jumped off the catwalk. No sooner had the last of us stepped off—Sammy—than we noticed the crazy boat had slipped silently away and was far down the canal, heading back to the lake and some other faraway place.

"Uh… where's he going?" Sammy asked with concern.

"We're on our own now," Gerty said. "Hammerling has business with Goji."

"With Goji?" I said with surprise. "Hammerling?"

"Why, of course," said Gerty. "Hammerling and Grimlo are two of the most trusted gnomes in the entire realm. Goji trusts the brothers with his most important tasks."

"Brothers?" my friends and I said at the same time. "Hammerling and Grimlo are brothers?"

"Why, of course," Gerty said. "You didn't see the resemblance?"

"Well, that explains a lot," Sammy said. And we all nodded. Yes, that explained a lot.

THE STONE
MAIDEN

"Chip-chop, off we go," said Gerty.

We followed her lead, occasionally hopping from one side of the path to the other. There must be booby traps here as well, I thought. Which also meant that we must be coming to the eastern edge of the gargoyle realm. I wasn't sure what we'd find beyond it.

As we walked, I felt like we were moving deeper and deeper into a living painting. The wavy watercolor shapes hovered in the air just beyond the streetlamps. I remembered seeing a painting in the museum called *Starry Night* by Vincent Van Gogh. Everything in the painting, the stars and sky, were mishappen and weird. It looked like a dream. And that's what the landscape looked like just beyond the streetlamps. It seemed like nothing real was out there beyond the light, only someone's crazy dream.

Our only company was the tall, quiet lamp posts casting out their magical light. But something was changing. It was definitely getting darker.

"Oh man," Sammy said, looking up at the sky with his special goggles. "I can't see the Snarlok path from here."

"You mean they lost our trail?" Kat asked.

"I don't know if they lost our trail, or if I lost theirs," said Sammy. "With this weird light it's hard to tell if it's day or night."

Sammy was right. The sky showed a strange twilight. And even though we knew it was getting later in the evening, because of Suzy's watch, it felt like it was eternal dawn here—the kind of twilight that happens right before the sun comes up.

"Oh no," Suzy said, just as her watch alarm went off. "We're out of time! We have to turn back."

"We've come too far to turn back now," said Gerty. "Besides, there's a bit of cushion in our deadline."

"A little bit," Suzy said, "but the way time works over here, I can't be sure if it will speed up or slow down on our return."

"Oh, I have faith in you," Gerty said. "You'll figure it out."

Suzy gave a surprised look and glanced at each one of us. Then she quickly went back to her book of clues.

"Hey, what's that?" said Kat.

We all stopped and looked to where she was pointing. The image of a statue had emerged from the strange twilight. It was a statue of a lady, carved from white marble. She was looking down into the water, silently waiting for something. But her actual image seemed to be made from light, like a reflection. The sparkling rays of rainbow light swirled around her image like a protective cloud. Shades of silver and gold clung to her, giving her form. She glowed with ghostly light.

As we walked closer, we saw a large ring of stones which surrounded her and held a shallow pool of water. The image of the maiden floated above the water. She was beautiful and scary all at the same time.

We stopped around the ring and looked in. Here, the water in the pool looked impossibly deep, like it went all the way to another world.

"Now what?" whispered Suzy.

"What did Goji say?" asked Gerty.

Suzy flipped to the back pages of her field guide where she'd scribbled the strange message and read:

"Find the one, who stands alone / In the golden rays, on morning's stone / A question she'll ask, and answer you must / Look deep within, to those whom you trust."

"Well, she's certainly alone," said Sammy.

"Yeah, and in golden rays," Suzy added.

"But where's the stone?" I asked. "She's not really standing on anything. She's just an image."

"Yeah, you're right," said Sammy. He walked a little closer to the ring of stones, adjusting his goggles. "She's just kind of— Ow!"

His knee banged into the edge of the stone circle, and he fell forward.

"Hey!" yelled Kat, grabbing him just before he tumbled into the water. She held the back of his shirt as he dangled out over the water.

After several seconds of arm-flailing, he said, "Hey, guys, look at this!"

We all leaned forward over the edge of the stones and peered into the water. At first, we couldn't see anything, then slowly an image formed.

"She's in the water," Kat whispered.

"Yeah, like upside-down in the water," I said.

"But how is that possible?" Suzy asked.

"And she's standing on a stone!" Sammy said.

"Wait, what?" Suzy said, and peered harder. "But that's not possible. Stones can't float, and certainly not upside down."

"Maybe not," Sammy shrugged, "but there she is. Wow. A stone maiden."

"Holy cow," I said. "I know what's happening."

"What?" everyone asked together.

"She's not upside down. She's standing on a stone, in a pool of water, in a courtyard somewhere. You know, like those old-time fountains. Her image is reflecting into the water and that's what we're seeing here, her image. We're the ones who are upside down, compared to her."

"We're upside down?" Sammy asked.

"Maybe," I said.

Everyone stood up and stared around the circle, looking at each other. We were silent for a long time, wondering if this could be true. It was almost too crazy to imagine.

"OK…" Suzy started. "You might be right, in a weird way. But why did Goji send us to her? She's not a gargoyle."

"Why do you think that?" Gerty asked. "All gargoyles don't have to have wings and fangs."

"You mean—?" Sammy started. "You mean there are beautiful gargoyles as well?"

"Well, of course," Gerty said. "She's quite marvelous, is she not?"

"I'll say," Sammy said. "So does that mean all the cool statues in museums are gargoyles, too?"

"No," Gerty said. "Not all statues are gargoyles, the same as not all gargoyles are ugly. But you'd be surprised where a gargoyle may turn up."

Whoa! I definitely had to be more careful what I said around my mom's planters, I thought. Who could tell when a plain old piece of concrete might be spying on you.

Then the stone maiden spoke, her voice rippling from the water. "The one you seek, is near and far, sailing on a shooting star."

Then she said, "What do I mean?"

We all looked at each other again.

"Wait, what?" I asked. "Is that it?"

The stone maiden was silent.

"Don't we get more of a hint than that?" Sammy asked, pushing his goggles up and rubbing his eyes.

"It's another riddle," said Suzy. "We have to figure it out."

"Oh, man," I said. "If I knew we were going to have this many pop quizzes, I would've stayed home."

"Milo!" Suzy said. "Seriously? We're talking about your uncle."

"I know, I know," I said. "But couldn't we get a normal hint, just once? Riddle me this, riddle me that, watch out for boogers at the end of a bat. Or something like that."

"That's not a riddle," Sammy said. "It's just a rhyme. But a good one!" He pretended to flick a booger off his finger.

"Time check." This time it was Kat who said it. "We're wasting time, you guys. Come on. Hurry up and solve the riddle."

"Let's ask Gerty," I said. And just then, we heard a faint snoring sound. Gerty had fallen asleep!

"Oh man!" I said. "Not now, Gerty! What do we do?"

"Focus," said Suzy.

"Yeah, Milo," Sammy said. "Focus a little, why don't you?" He chuckled to himself. "Do the crazy hand thing. Maybe it'll come to you."

"I wish," I said. "But it doesn't exactly work that way."

Suzy continued. "'The one you seek.' That's easy. The stone maiden is talking about Milo's uncle, Horace. I think."

We all agreed that she was right. Probably.

"Is near and far," Suzy continued. "How can someone be near and far at the same time?"

We all scuffed our sneakers on the cobblestones, thinking.

"Come on," Suzy said, "hurry up you guys. It's almost 7:45. We're late."

"Well," I said, "sometimes in class, when I'm daydreaming, Ms. Halsey my teacher would say, 'Earth to Milo, come in, Milo.' My mind was kind of far away at those times, although I was sitting right there."

"That's it!" said Kat. "Someone is 'near and far' when they're daydreaming! Their body is near, but their mind is far away."

"Yeah, or when they're asleep and dreaming for real," said Sammy. "Dreaming of being on a shooting star!"

A BOY IN THE WATER

"So Milo's uncle is trapped in a dream or something?" Kat said. "But where?"

"I don't know if he's trapped," I said. "Maybe he's just asleep. Maybe the Snarloks cast a sleeping spell on him."

Just then, we heard another voice from the pool of water. But it wasn't the voice of the maiden. It was a boy's voice. He had a speech impediment, and his words came out slow and thick. "Hey, how'd you get in dere?" he asked. "Not 'posed to pway in da wata. Might dwown."

His voice came out watery and garbled, but we could understand him.

We all leaned over the edge of the pool and looked into the water. There, on the other side, where the stone maiden stood atop her majestic stone, was the image of a boy. He was standing, looking down into the pool of water from his side, seeing us looking back. He had a flat face and kind eyes. He cracked a wide smile and waved at us. We waved back in surprise.

"Whoa!" I said. "Am I really seeing this?"

"Who is that?" Sammy asked. "And *where* is that? It's like a whole 'nother world over there."

"Well," said Suzy, "why wouldn't it be? We came through a gate on Gargoyle Hill. Apparently, this gate goes through the fountain, guarded by the stone maiden, and comes out in a courtyard somewhere."

"Ah you 'tuck?" the boy in the water said.

"No, we're not stuck," I said to the boy. "But we're looking for my uncle. Do you know where he is?"

The boy scrunched his face, scratched his head, then asked, "Is he in dere?"

"No," I said. "He's not in here." I thought that was a silly question, but I knew he was just trying to help. The boy reminded me of someone in my grade who went to gifted classes. Then I realized that his question wasn't that silly after all. We were in the realm of the gargoyles specifically to look for my uncle. So, in a way, the boy's question was actually valid.

"Well, he's probably in here," I said, "just… not right *here*. If that makes any sense. Anyway, my name is Milo. What's yours?"

The boy's smile widened even further. "Yimmy," he said. "Yimmy Wawoo." And thumbed his chest.

"I think he's saying 'Jimmy,'" Suzy said.

"Yeah," Sammy agreed. "But I've never heard of the last name of Wawoo."

"I don't think he can pronounce his L's," Suzy whispered. "And maybe not his R's."

"Where do you live, Jimmy?" Suzy asked.

"At Ahman's," Jimmy said.

We stared at each other and shrugged.

"Which city is that in?" Suzy asked again.

At this, Jimmy scrunched his face in thought. "Ummm…" he said. Then shrugged his shoulders. "I fohgot."

Then Kat spoke up. "Hey guys, ticking clock, remember? Let's hurry this thing up!"

"Oh, man," I said. "Sorry Jimmy, but we really have to go and—"

"Wait you guys," Suzy said. "We can't leave yet."

We all leaned back from the pool. From this position, we could see the maiden's reflection hovering above the water on our side, but couldn't see Jimmy.

Sammy's eyes bugged out. "What do you mean we can't leave yet? What about the ticking clock, Grimlo's warning, the Snarloks?" He danced from side to side like he had to pee.

"I know, Sammy," Suzy said. "And I'm watching the time, but Goji sent us here for a reason, to talk to the stone maiden. We think. But what if we were supposed to find Jimmy as well?"

We all looked at each other with puzzled faces. It sounded plausible. But if that was the case, why hadn't Goji just said so? Then I realized that this sounded like something a tricky gargoyle would do.

"But," I whispered, "Jimmy doesn't… well… doesn't sound like… you know… like he knows very much."

"Milo!" Suzy said. "That's not nice, and he can't help it!"

"I know, I know," I said. "I'm not trying to be mean. He seems like a nice kid and all, I'm just not sure he can help us."

"Well, maybe we're not asking him the right questions," said Suzy. "After all, he answered your first question correctly, didn't he?"

"Not really," I said. "I mean, he asked me if Uncle Horace was in here. That wasn't a real answer."

"But we are in *here* looking for him," she said.

"Yeah, but that was a lucky answer," I said. Then thought again. "And it wasn't even a real answer anyway."

"But," Kat said, "we didn't hear Jimmy's voice until AFTER we figured out the maiden's riddle. Goji told us we had to answer her question. And we did. Maybe it was a test. And once we passed the test, by answering her question, we were able to hear Jimmy. Or… something like that."

"Hey," Sammy said, "actually, that's not a bad idea." He stood there, rubbing his chin and nodding to himself as if he'd just thought of it.

Kat huffed and crossed her arms. Her lips were tight, and she spoke between her teeth. "If either one of you say, 'Actually Kat, that's not a bad idea,' to me one more time, you're getting clobbered! Clan or no clan."

YIKES! Sammy and I looked at each other, then muttered, "… sorry."

"I'm going to try anyway," Suzy said. "Just a few more minutes." Then leaned over and looked into the water.

We all looked in and watched.

"Hi, Jimmy," said Suzy. "Would you like to play a game?"

Jimmy's eyes lit up. "Ah, game? I'm good at games."

"OK, great. If we were to play Hide and Seek in here, where would we hide?"

One side of Jimmy's face scrunched up and a nostril flared. He looked like he'd just smelled something stinky, or didn't understand the question. Finally, he said, "In da dawk?"

Suzy nodded. "Yeah, me too. I'd hide in the dark. But do you know of any special places in here, in the dark, where someone would hide?"

"Mmmm… a cwoset," Jimmy said.

Suzy looked surprised. "A closet? In the water?"

Jimmy's face scrunched again. "Not in da' wata. You cwothes get wet."

"But I don't understand," said Suzy. "Where is the closet, if it's not in the water?"

"My woom," Jimmy said.

Suzy leaned back from the pool and looked at us. "I'm confused. I don't think this is working. How could there be a closet, or his room, in the water?"

"It's not in the water," I said. "Jimmy looks like *he's* in the water to us, but we look the same to him. He's looking into a pool, seeing our reflections, just like we're looking in and seeing his. None of us are actually wet though."

"Actually," Kat said with a wry smile, "that's not a half bad idea, Milo." She crossed her arms and smirked at me.

OK, I thought. I deserved that one.

"Oh, man," said Sammy. "This is super weird. I should totally write a book about this someday."

"OK, you're right," Suzy said to me. "But I asked Jimmy where someone would hide, in HERE. Not out THERE in his world. The closet in his room can't be in HERE. Can it?"

I shrugged and said, "At this point anything is possible, I guess. Ask him."

We looked at each other and shrugged. *Why not?* was the unspoken message.

Then we all leaned over and looked back into the water.

A HIDDEN
ROOM

Jimmy was waiting patiently. During the time we'd been talking, he'd knelt by the pool and was leaning his elbows on the stone ring. He watched us closely.

"Jimmy," Suzy said. "What does your room look like?"

Jimmy thought about this for a minute, then smiled. "It got a bed dat goes 'ike dis, bounce, bounce, bounce." He bobbed his head around as if he were bouncing on his mattress. "And a winnow where da biwd talks to me."

"The what?" Suzy asked suddenly. "A window where a bird talks to you?"

"Yeah," Jimmy said.

"Wow, he must be a smart bird if he can talk."

Jimmy shrugged. "Yeah, he puwty smart I guess."

"What else?"

"Da mirrow where Victah lives."

"A mirror? And someone named Victor lives in it?"

"Yeah."

"Does Victor talk to you too?"

"Yeah, but he's seepin' now."

Suzy glanced at us with wide eyes. It sounded like Jimmy lived in a haunted house!

"What else?" she asked. "Is there a closet in your room?"

"Uh huh, Sinky lives dere."

"Sinky?" Suzy asked.

"Syyinky..." Jimmy tried.

"Slinky?"

"Yeah."

"And what is Slinky?"

"He da shadow in my cwoset," Jimmy said. "He goes 'ike dis." Jimmy pointed his finger and moved it back and forth, like a slinking, slithering snake. Then he covered his mouth with his other hand and whispered strange noises into it. It sounded like a made-up language.

"What's that sound you're making?" Suzy asked. "It sounds scary."

"It's Sinky, he goes 'ike dis, *whisper, whisper, whisper.*"

A cold chill ran down my back when Jimmy said that. I suddenly had the idea that he was describing a Snarlok ghost tentacle, but didn't know it. Now I was afraid that the Snarloks were living in Jimmy's house. Maybe even in his room!

Then I had an idea.

"Hey, Jimmy," I said. "Can you concentrate really hard and think about what your room looks like?"

Suzy looked at me with a question on her face but said nothing.

I held up one finger, telling her to wait.

Jimmy scrunched his face again, then closed his eyes. He was deep in concentration. We waited for several seconds, then suddenly Sammy spoke.

"Uh, guys," he whispered. "Guys. Are you seeing this?"

We looked up. Sammy was pointing to something about ten feet beyond the reflection of the stone maiden. The air, which still looked like a watercolor background, had begun to swirl. It looked like someone was mixing paints on a giant easel, but with an invisible paint brush. The colors swirled and mixed for several seconds. I thought they were going to turn into a muddy brown color, but they didn't. They started to form a picture. Somehow, the swirling paints formed lines and edges, and the image of a room appeared in the mist.

"What is that?" whispered Suzy.

"A ghost room?" whispered Sammy.

"No," whispered Kat. "I think that's Jimmy's room."

"How is he doing that?" Sammy whispered. "He's projecting the image of his room to us!"

We were all whispering because we didn't want to disturb Jimmy's concentration.

We stood and watched as the image became clearer. We saw the bed that Jimmy had described. From the view of the bed, his bedroom door was on the right. The window was on the left. There was a chest of drawers at the end of the bed with a mirror on it. That must have been where Victor lived.

CREEPY!

Then we saw the bedroom door open, and Jimmy walk into the room. He closed the door behind him and stood facing the mirror at the end of the bed.

I peeked over the ledge of stones and saw Jimmy's reflection in the water, so I knew he was still kneeling at the edge of the pool. And, he still had his eyes closed. But from our side, it looked like he was standing in his room. "Jimmy," I whispered towards the water, "we can see your room."

Suddenly, the Jimmy in the room turned around and looked at the wall where the headboard of his bed was. A funny look came over his face, then he cracked a smile. He squinted, looked harder, then smiled some more. Then he waved at us! Somehow, while thinking about his own room, and projecting its image into our world, he could see us as if he was looking at us through the wall.

"Jimmy," I said quietly, "can you show us your closet?"

He nodded, but put one finger to his lips. Showing us that we should be quiet. Then he turned and walked toward the end of the bed. As he did, our view followed him, as if we were walking behind him. He walked around the end of the bed. The closet door sat to the left of his dresser. He put his hand on the doorknob, then looked back at us again. In the vision, his mouth moved, but we heard his words come out of the water. "Watch out for Sinky. Don't wake him up."

Then he turned the knob and opened the closet door.

A SNARLOK TRAP

In the gargoyle realm, behind the reflection of the stone maiden, a door opened in the watercolor mist. The ghostly, painted image of Jimmy stood outside the door, watching us.

"Do we go in?" Sammy asked.

"We have to," said Kat. "We're almost out of time."

"But what about Gerty?" he asked. "She's still asleep."

"We'll just go in and take a quick look," Kat said. "Gerty will be fine right there."

Sammy looked alarmed. "What are you talking about?" he said. "We can't leave her."

"Oh, come on," said Kat. "You're just stalling because you're afraid to go in."

"No I'm not!" Sammy said.

"OK then, after you." And Kat motioned for Sammy to take the lead.

Sammy turned and gulped at me. "Uh, Milo," he said, "well... he's your uncle after all."

"Alright," I said. "Come on." And we walked through the door, with me in the lead.

Inside, a strange light radiated out of the walls. It smelled dusty (like old closets do) and was packed with boxes. Old coats and sweaters hung from wires strung along the ceiling.

"Kinda creepy," Sammy started.

I spun around quickly with my finger to my lips. We had to be quiet.

Sammy mouthed his response. *Sorry.*

The closet went back and back. It was much bigger than it looked. Soon we saw a door on the opposite wall. That was weird, I thought. I'd never seen a closet with more than one door. Then I noticed another door, and another. The closet seemed to stretch between multiple bedrooms, and was used by all of them. That explained all the junk.

I crept forward, wondering if my footsteps in this world would creak old wooden floorboards in Jimmy's world. I was totally improvising. Again.

A little further in and I heard a faint snoring sound coming from beneath one of the doors. I motioned to my friends what I was hearing and that we needed to go on.

We crept further into the closet, listening at each door. There were six doors in total, and we heard snoring coming from three of them.

That was weird, I thought. How many sleeping people were in this house, anyway?

Suzy scribbled a note and passed it around.

How do we choose? It read.

I shrugged again. I'd only been at my uncle's house for one lousy night. I didn't even know IF he snored, much less what it sounded like.

Then an idea came to me.

I pulled my Moonstone necklace out from beneath my shirt and motioned for the others to do the same. Maybe the talismans could tell us something.

Quietly, we all gathered by one door and watched the colors of our necklaces. By the first door, they didn't change color at all. Then we went to the second door. At first nothing happened, but then slowly, the Moonstones began to pulse. A very faint red.

Oh no! I thought, then stopped. Hey, is it turning red, or is that kind of purple? Oh man, I couldn't tell!

I motioned everyone on to the third door and waited. Here the Moonstones turned a faint shade of blue.

Blue was safe, wasn't it? We all looked at Suzy.

For a second, she wasn't sure what we were looking at. She wrinkled her face in confusion. Then I pointed at my talisman, then at the third door, then at her book. I shrugged. *Is it safe to go in?*

She held up one finger, then began flipping through her field guide. Finally, after what seemed like forever, she stopped on a page, scanned it, and nodded. Then turned to show us the page.

Written in pencil with shaky handwriting were Uncle Horace's notes on what the Moonstone colors meant.

Blue light means safety (except when it's raining)

Red light means Snarloks (depending on the direction of the wind)

Yellow light means be careful when walking (unless you're running)

Black light means something good or bad. It just depends.

Then at the very bottom of the page were these words:

Your guess is as good as mine.

WHAT?

I grabbed my head in frustration. *Come on, Uncle Horace,* I thought, *we could use some better instructions than that!*

Suzy shrugged and pointed at me. It was my decision.

I nodded my head and turned towards the third door. It was here the Moonstone light had been sort of bluish.

I grabbed the doorknob and slowly turned. The latch clicked and the door swung open. The room was so junky it was hard to focus on one thing. But I quickly saw what I was looking for.

There was Uncle Horace!

And he *was* asleep, just like we'd thought. He was leaning back in an old dusty recliner, but instead of snoring, he was mumbling.

Wait a minute! I thought. *This is too easy. It must be a trap.*

I motioned to Sammy to come forward. He crept up slowly. I pointed for him to put his goggles on and see if there was anything hidden in the closet.

He nodded his head in understanding and began to scan the room. After a few seconds he turned and gave me a thumbs up.

I tiptoed into the room and reached for my uncle's shoulder. Just then Sammy grabbed my shoulders from behind.

I spun around and saw a giant set of eyes staring back at me. He was pointing frantically behind my uncle's head.

"What?" I said.

"Tentacle!" Sammy yelled.

I looked back at my uncle and saw what Sammy was pointing at. What I thought was an old vacuum cleaner hose hanging from the wall was really a tentacle. It had been hidden amongst the junk in the room and was attached to my uncle's head. I watched in disgust as the slimy thing slowly massaged his head. With each squeeze of its tentacle my uncle's mouth moved. He wasn't just murmuring in his sleep. He had been hypnotized! The Snarloks had hypnotized him and were massaging the secret of the Moonstone right out of his head!

"Uncle Horace!" I screamed. "Wake up!" And I leapt forward, grabbing the tentacle with my hands.

He let out a loud snort and his eyes fluttered. "Wha?" he mumbled.

Something behind the wall hissed as the tentacle flailed in the air. Its poisonous skin burned my hands, but I held on. I screamed at it for what it had done to Uncle Horace and tried to rip it to pieces. But this wasn't a small tentacle, nor a weak one, and it nearly overpowered me.

We were locked in a deadly embrace.

When Uncle Horace started awake his left hand flew open. And the rest of the Snarlok trap was revealed.

A small marble had been tucked into his hand. When he woke up his hand opened, and the marble dropped out. It bounced a few times on the old wood floor and rolled towards the wall—the wall shared by the room where the Moonstone had turned red. The room I thought might be hiding more Snarloks.

I was still wrestling with the tentacle and watched as the marble rolled across the floor, then through a mouse hole in the baseboard. It went straight into the Snarlok room. Somewhere in the other room I heard the marble roll to a stop with the faintest *clink*. It had hit something glass, but barely made a sound.

Then everything happened at once.

We heard glass break. Then something fell over. A whistle blew and a metal mop bucket clanged to the floor. I imagined a crazy pile of objects—like dominos—all stacked together, waiting to fall over and make a tremendous noise. It was a Snarlok trap, after all. The marble had set it off. And now the things in the closet were starting to wake up.

"RRRAAAWWWWW!" something growled from the other room.

And we knew we were in trouble.

THINGS GO FROM BAD TO WORSE

Snarlok tentacles slithered out of the walls and across the ceiling. They were trying to block our path out.

I released the tentacle I was wrestling with, grabbed Uncle Horace and pulled him to his feet. "Come on!" I yelled. "Uncle Horace, wake up!"

He staggered to his feet, half awake. "Wha?" he tried to say. "Wha's happening? Mii-llo, is that you?"

Kat yelled from the main closet. "Get back you slimy Snarlok!" She was waving an arrow back and forth at the ceiling, trying to keep the tentacles from closing off our escape route.

We ran for the door of Jimmy's closet. Kat first, then Suzy and Sammy. I followed with Uncle Horace.

Just then, a dark shadow slipped out from beneath one of the other doors. It lay across the closet floor like a thick puddle of tar.

"Look out!" yelled Sammy. "It's Slinky!"

As Sammy yelled out its name, Slinky the shadow struck like a snake and lashed onto Kat's ankle.

"Ow!" she cried and dropped her arrow. "It burns!" She tried to pull her leg away, but Slinky held tight. "Ow! Help!" She scrambled to grab another arrow from the quiver strung over her back.

"Let me," said Suzy, and grabbed an arrow from Kat's quiver. With one quick movement, she thrust it into the black shadow on the floor. It had the same effect as it did on the Snarlok tentacles. The shadow cried out.

"AHHYEEEEEE," the shadow hissed and let go of Kat's ankle.

"Now jump!" yelled Suzy as she grabbed Kat's arm. Kat jumped over the shadow, holding onto Suzy for support.

Suzy continued to stab at the shadow on the floor, forcing it back under the door. Kat pulled another arrow and shot it into the biggest tentacle sliding out of the ceiling. The Snarlok growled and hissed from behind the door. Then Kat tossed arrows to me and Sammy.

We ran from the closet, waving arrows at anything that moved. We tumbled out of the imaginary room and fell to the ground near the edge of the pool of water.

Stunned, we all looked around to make sure no one was hurt. Kat was rubbing her ankle, but stopped when she saw us looking at her. "It's nothing," she said quickly. "I've had worse rope burns."

"Are we safe?" Sammy asked. "Did we escape?"

"I think so," I said.

Then we heard it. The alarm of Suzy's watch. It had been beeping for a while, but with all the commotion we hadn't heard it.

"Oh no, no," Suzy said. "This can't be right."

"What now?" I asked.

"It can't be right," she said again. "My watch says it's 10:30!"

We don't have enough time to get back!"

"10:30?" Sammy asked. "Is it broken?"

"No," Uncle Horace spoke up. "It ain't broken. Those tricky Snarloks have been messin' with the Sands of Time again."

"The what?" I asked.

"The Sands of Time," he repeated. "Silas has been settin' traps for me for years, but this one is a doozy! Tricky, tricky!"

"But how do we get back?" I asked. "Grimlo said—"

"I know what Grimlo said," Uncle Horace replied. "Somethin' vurry bad is about to happen."

"GGRRAAAHHHHGGGG!!!"

A terrible growl emerged from the mist where Jimmy's room had been. It was so loud it vibrated the rainbow light that floated around us. The light shook so hard I thought it was going to shatter into a thousand pieces.

"We have to go right now!" yelled Suzy. "I think I remember the way back, but— oh no! The lake! And the canal! We don't have a boat. We're trapped!"

Uncle Horace shook his head. "Not yet, we're not! There's something I need to do!"

He staggered to the edge of the pool, then peered in.

"B... but wh-what's going to happen?" asked Sammy. "My p-parents are going to be really m-mad if I get squooshed."

Uncle Horace turned and looked at me. "I know you ain't ready boy, but there's only one way we're getting' out of here."

"What is it?" I asked.

"FIGHT!" And he pointed at the Snarlok behind me.

THE FIGHT OF
OUR LIVES

I turned just in time to see a Snarlok walk out of the mist. It wasn't just a tentacle, and they weren't just partially formed. Somehow the Snarloks had found their way back into the gargoyle realm, and one was standing right in front of me.

It stood as tall as my uncle, but walked on powerful legs that ended in claws. Its arms bulged with muscles and ended in clawed hands. It had the head of an octopus, with large watery eyes. Instead of wings, large tentacles came out of its back.

Uncle Horace leaned over the stone circle and yelled into the water. "Jimmy! You there boy?"

"Incoming!" Sammy yelled, pointing at the sky. He was looking through his goggles. "More Snarloks!"

We looked up and saw them at the same time. Red meteor streaks in the sky, high above us. It looked like the Snarloks were coming from all directions. They were surrounding us in the mist. This must have been their plan all along. After the marble-alarm went off, they just had to stall us long enough for more of them to get here. We were doomed.

"Jimmy? You there boy?" Horace yelled again.

"Quick, form a circle," I said. "We'll hold them off as long as we can."

We formed a circle around the pool of water. Kat had her bow and arrow drawn. Sammy was tracking the Snarloks with his goggles. We all held arrows out in front of us.

"We're the Savage clan!" I yelled. "We are Gargoyle Hunters! And Snarloks cannot pass!"

Just then, a brilliant flash of red light shot out of our talismans. The red light hovered in front of each of us for a second, then arced across to the next person. It looked like small bolts of lightning reaching from one person to the next. Soon, a ring of red light connected us. We were the lightning rods. And we were truly a clan.

The Snarloks hissed and fell back. Some of them shielded their eyes from the bright glare. But none of them left. They were waiting for something.

We heard Jimmy's voice from the water. "Hi, Howace! You was seepin'."

"Yeah, I was sleepin' alright," Horace said. "But now I need to get back home, and I mean quick-quick."

"Maybe you wun fast," Jimmy said.

"No," Horace said, "faster than that. Can you whip me up a whirlpool?"

"Tentacle at twelve o'clock," Sammy yelled, and pointed over Kat's head.

With ninja-like reflexes, Kat shot an arrow straight up over her head, piercing the tip of a tentacle. They were still trying to get us despite the protective ring of light.

"Quick-quick now Jimmy," Horace said. "And make it a big one!"

I looked into the water and saw Jimmy crack a wide smile. His eyes glistened. "I make it a BIG one!" he said. Then he leaned out over the stones in his world, stuck his hand in the water, and began to swirl it in a large, clockwise motion.

The effect was almost instantaneous. A wind began to blow in the gargoyle realm.

I looked at the sky, which now was deep night, sprinkled with stars. I didn't see any storm clouds. But a storm was coming. I could feel it in the wind.

"Four o'clock!" Sammy yelled, directing our attention. "Nine and ten!"

With each warning from Sammy, we all jabbed at tentacles, barely keeping the Snarloks back.

I looked back into the water and watched as Jimmy swirled his hand faster and faster in that magical pool of water. As the water swirled in his world, the wind blew harder in ours. And the whole time, the beautiful stone maiden stood on her stone and watched it all. She may have been the guardian of the Easterling gate, but Jimmy was its keeper. I was sure of that now.

"Keep it going, Jimmy!" Uncle Horace yelled. "It's blowin' a good one!"

Jimmy nodded his head and smiled. He swirled his hand faster.

"Come on kids!" Horace said. "Gather together so you don't get blowed away!"

We all surrounded Uncle Horace. The ring of red light moving with us.

"I can barely stand up!" yelled Suzy. "How are we supposed to get back now? We can't run in this."

"Milo, grab 'ole Gerty," Horace said. "She'll wake up in a minute. She don't like no wind in her ears."

I tossed my arrow to Kat, then picked up Gerty. I almost got blown over myself, then stumbled back to the group.

"RRRAAAAHHHHHRRRRRRGGGGG!"

The loudest, most terrible sound we'd ever heard came roaring through the wind. But we knew it wasn't the wind. And it wasn't any old Snarlok.

Silas, the chief of the Snarlok clan, was coming towards us.

A KITE
IN FLIGHT

Looking into the swirling mist, I saw the outline of a huge creature, ten feet tall, and wider than Goji. It was a giant, fat thing that lumbered on huge legs. It was Silas.

The head of an octopus and a beak mouth came into view. Giant red tentacles stuck out of its back and flailed at the air. Huge claws crushed the ground with each step.

"Silas!" I yelled. "He got in! He's coming for us!"

"I thought he was banished?" Suzy yelled to Uncle Horace. The wind was so loud now, we could barely hear each other.

"Aye, he was," Horace yelled back. "But we ain't stickin' around to ask how he got back in. Thanks again, Jimmy!" he yelled into the water. "Now follow me!"

And he ran into the mist where the room had just been.

Kat, Suzy and Sammy surrounded me as I carried Gerty. They stabbed at tentacles as we went.

The wind almost blew us over several times. Suzy's explorer hat flew off her head and disappeared into the mist. Sammy wobbled back and forth with his arms out and almost went rolling away. Kat leaned sideways into the wind, grunting as she fought to stand. She turned occasionally and sent an arrow flying back towards Silas, who was still lumbering after us.

We stumbled forward like this for several minutes, until we suddenly crashed into the back of Uncle Horace.

"Up you go," he said. And one by one, he pushed us up onto a stone step where a strong pair of hands pulled us even higher.

It was Hammerling!

"Ahoy there!" he bellowed. "You look like you be needed some assistance."

"What took ya so long?" Horace asked. "Nappin' in the pixie fields, were ya?"

"Aye… weren't nappin' Horace," Hammerling said. "I was headin' out to Westworld when I felt the wind change. Had to pull out me trusty kite-sail to get here this fast."

Gerty was still sleeping, so we had to lift her onto Hammerling's boat of crates. I didn't realize there was another canal this far out, but he'd gotten his boat here somehow.

"The wind is too fierce for the upper deck," Hammerling yelled. "Best you all stay down here!"

"Grab the railing!" Horace called. "It's gonna be a bumpy ride!"

We all grabbed onto the thin railing that ran around the catwalk at the bottom of the boat. I still couldn't see any water and wondered how we'd escape with a boat on dry land.

BOINGG!

Then Hammerling sprung up the side of the crates like a mountain goat.

More tentacles came out of the air and snatched at the sides of the boat. They caught the ropes that held the crates together and began to pull. They were trying to untie them and pull the boat apart!

"Oh no you don't!" Hammerling yelled. "No Snarlok is gonna mess with MY boat!"

Then Hammerling pulled a lever and a small canon went off. It shot a projectile into the air which suddenly burst open like a parachute. The wind caught it and it ballooned into the biggest kite I'd ever seen. It was a kite-sail!

The boat jerked and flew off in an instant. Sammy stumbled from the sudden movement and almost flew off the catwalk. He grabbed the rail just in time and pulled himself back on.

Silas roared in anger behind us as the magic wind pulled us from the Snarlok's grip.

If the first boat ride was harrowing, this one was downright terrifying. The magic wind that Jimmy had created with his whirlpool blew the little boat at a crazy speed. Hammerling swung from rope to rope above us, yelling instructions to himself.

"Stow the mizzy-thing and shorten that blabber-sail!" Captain Hammerling called.

"Aye-aye, captain," First Mate Hammerling responded, and swung to another rope.

The boat rocked from side to side, nearly tipping over several times. Images of Snarloks flew past us in the mist, mostly reaching out for us with their sticky tentacles just a little too late. Occasionally, an unlucky Snarlok would manage to grab hold of a rope, only to have the end of their tentacles torn off, due to how fast we were moving. There were so many tentacles stuck to the ropes of Hammerling's boat, we looked like a flying plate of calamari!

We caught glimpses of the outer edge of Easterling as we sailed past it. Tall columns of mist announced the arrival of more gargoyles. There must have been hundreds of gargoyles coming to palaver.

Garden gnomes hurried along stone and water paths, moving their goods. And somewhere far to our right, I thought I could see the center of the realm where Goji would preside over all the gargoyle clans. Minus the Snarloks, of course.

Uncle Horace came over to me. "Come with me," he whispered. Then he walked around the catwalk.

On the other side of the boat, he waited for me.

"What is it?" I asked. "What's wrong?"

He leaned down and whispered in my ear. "You did well back there, my boy. Very brave of you to stand up to the Snarloks."

"Thanks," I said.

"Mayhap a bit foolish… but brave as well. Things are happening quickly now. I thought we'd have more time."

"More time for what?" I asked.

"Your training, of course. But I fear we're out of time. And if something vurry bad were to happen… well, you should know the secret."

I looked at him in surprise. "The secret?" I said. "Of the—"

"Shh!" he whispered, then leaned closer. "Yes. The secret of the Moonstone. You need to know it. Just in case. But you can never tell it. Can you promise to do that?"

I thought back to all the goof-ups and trouble I'd caused in the past. I couldn't believe this responsibility had come to me. I still wasn't sure I was the right person for the job. But my mom had always believed in me. She said one day I'd find what I was good at. Maybe this was it.

I looked at my uncle. Maybe it was my imagination, but at that moment he reminded me of my mom. Just a little. And I thought he had the same look of pride on his face that I sometimes saw on hers.

"Yes," I whispered. "I promise to keep the secret."

My uncle smiled and clasped my shoulders. "Now listen closely," he said. "There is a silver key hidden in my den. Only Grimlo and I know where it is. On the day of the Gargoyle Moon, you take the silver key up to the Well House on Gargoyle Hill. Inside the Well House you'll see a grate covering the well. Unlock the grate with the key, then open it. Next, you'll speak these words three times: *Prodire Selene*." He pronounced it pro-dear-ee sa-lean-ee.

"What does it mean?" I asked.

"It means, *Come forth, Selene*."

"But what is Selene?"

"Selene is the proper name of the Moonstone. Its ancient name. It's how you wake it up. Once you wake it up, the gargoyles can palaver."

I swelled with pride knowing that I'd just been trusted with the secret.

"Thanks, Uncle Horace," I said. "I won't let you down."

I rejoined my friends on the other side of the boat. They seemed to know that something special had passed between me and my uncle, but didn't ask.

After a while, the wind began to slow and soon we bumped to a stop on a cobblestone path. Apparently, we hadn't been on a water canal at all. Then I realized that we probably had been flying in the air this whole time.

"All ashore!" Hammerling called and swung down on a rope. "Now, that weren't so bad, aye?"

"Not bad at all," Uncle Horace said. "Quite top notch."

"I say," Gerty yawned. "Are we home already, dears?"

"Gerty!" I said. "You're awake!"

"Well of course I am," she said, yawning again. "I just closed my eyes for a wink."

I knew dog years went fast compared to humans. But apparently, their naps weren't that way at all.

"The time!" yelled Suzy. "It's 11:49! We only have ten minutes!"

"Quick-quick, everyone!" Uncle Horace yelled. And he began to run again.

TIME IS UP

We ran down the stone path. The very same one Gerty had led us down earlier that day. But it didn't seem like it had only been a few hours. It felt like we'd been gone a long time. And now we had only a few minutes to make it back.

Uncle Horace jigged and jogged, stepping lightly over stones that were most likely traps. I kept looking back, expecting to see something coming out of the mist behind us, but nothing did. The path seemed familiar, but I couldn't understand how we'd gotten back here so quickly. I knew the magic wind had blown us at an incredible speed, but we'd been far out to the east and hadn't come back the same way. There was something very strange about how we'd traveled around the gargoyle realm.

Suddenly Uncle Horace cried out.

Up ahead, he'd just stepped off the last stone and onto the grassy field of Gargoyle Hill. There the fog swirled, just like when we'd left. But something was different.

"OWWW!" Uncle Horace cried. "Spickelarks!"

The cloud of fog rolled over and over as a thousand tiny birds attacked us. They plucked at our hair and clothes. They crashed into our heads. They even nipped at our arms. They were everywhere, and I suddenly imagined this must have been what it felt like when Mom was attacked by the plague of locusts. Then I was angry and sad all at the same time.

I reached down and tore up two large clumps of grass from the field and waved them over my head. I looked like a crazy scarecrow.

"Come on you stupid Spickelarks!" I yelled. "Come and get me!" And I ran out ahead of the group, trying to draw the birds away from them.

Below us, halfway down the hill, I saw the shimmering edge of the fog bank. The dry creek bed was just beyond it. We were almost home!

I was on the high side of the hill, drawing the Spickelarks up. Uncle Horace and the others were below me, heading straight for the creek. A lot of birds followed me, but there were still plenty harassing my friends.

"Ouch, ow, ouch!" Sammy cried. His arms flailed wildly over his head.

"Hi-YAH!

"Ho!

"Ha!

"Kee-YAH!"

Kat was karate-chopping at the annoying birds. She hit a surprising number of them, but still lost several strands of hair in the process.

"Come on, Milo!" Uncle Horace yelled up to me. "We'll all cross over together."

What a relief! I thought. I was tired of swinging my arms around like a monkey.

We all stepped through the wall of mist at the same time and stood at the edge of the creek. A crisp, clear night sky spread out over our heads. A few remaining Spickelarks dove at us, but most of them had stayed in the fog.

"Aarrrr… you wantin' to cause me a hearty-tack!" Grimlo yelled from the front porch. He was jumping up and down, causing the shutters to slam open and shut. "It's 11:57! RUN!"

We scrambled down the side of the creek bed and sprinted for the house.

Kat was the fastest and zoomed ahead of everyone, crossing the gravel driveway.

Suzy was close behind her.

"Ow, my ankle!" Sammy yelled. The ankle he'd twisted earlier gave out and sent him sprawling into the tall grass.

I ran to help him. I pulled him up and he leaned on my shoulder. We went hobbling across the driveway. His double-stacked goggles bouncing crazily on his head.

Kat crossed the yard and landed on the porch rail with a high jump. "Hi-Yah!" she yelled and clung to it like a monkey.

Suzy crossed the yard next and ran straight up the steps two at a time. She collapsed onto the porch. "I made it!"

"It's 11:58 and thirty seconds!" screamed Grimlo. "Hurry up!"

"Come on, you guys!" Kat shouted. "You can do it!"

"Quickly now, my dears!" Gerty shouted. "Don't tarry!"

"Hurry!" yelled Suzy. "You're almost there!"

It was an awesome sight to see my friends cheering us on. Even Grimlo had a look of encouragement on his face. In between yelling at us to hurry up, of course.

Uncle Horace caught up to me and Sammy. "Up you go." Then he grabbed Sammy's other arm and we practically carried him across the rest of the lawn.

We scurried up the steps and fell onto the porch, exhausted.

Everyone cheered.

We'd made it back!

WE CELEBRATE

"HURRAH!" Grimlo yelled. He went bouncing around the front porch.

BOINGG!

BOINGG!

"You did it!" Gerty said. "You ALL did it. Well done!"

"But we couldn't have done it without you Gerty," I said. "You led us."

Sammy sat on the porch rubbing his ankle. "And Milo figured out a lot of stuff. We all might have gotten squooshed without him."

"But you spotted the Snarloks in the sky," Suzy said to Sammy. "And you were really brave when we had to fight them off by the stone maiden."

"Good thing Kat's archery skills are ninja-level," I said. "We might not have made it out of the Snarlok trap without her."

"Well," Kat said from the railing, "Suzy played a big part in that. Thanks for fighting off Slinky when it grabbed my ankle."

"You're welcome," Suzy said. "I'm glad you're in the clan."

"That's right," I said. "We're truly a clan now. The Savage Clan!"

And everyone cheered again.

While we'd been talking, the remaining time on the owl clock had ticked down. Through the front window I saw the owl make a final pass around the room, then land back on its carved branch.

"Time is up," I said to everyone. "What happens now?"

Uncle Horace had been silent since we'd made it back, but now he looked at each of us. "First, I must express my sincerest gratitude to each of you. Without your brave actions, the tricky Snarloks may have gotten the secret of the Moonstone right out of my old noodle." And he tapped his head.

Grimlo and Horace spoke at the same time. "And that would be vurry bad."

Uncle Horace continued. "But we avoided disaster, and the palaver can continue. It's only a few days away!

"And as far as what we do now. Let's watch some magic." And he turned and looked out at the night sky.

I looked out across the yard. That's when I saw the vortex.

Out near the dry creek bed, floating in midair, was a weird column of air that was starting to spin.

It looked sort of like a small tornado or dust devil spinning up, only it was lying on its side. The air twisted and spun as it grew in size. I thought the Snarloks were about to pop out of the gargoyle realm again. But I was wrong. The vortex spun faster, then seemed to come to life. That's when the darkness started to disappear.

Like some weird, cosmic vacuum cleaner, the darkness of nighttime was being sucked up by the end of the vortex. And the more darkness the thing sucked up, the larger it grew, and the faster it spun.

All around the farmhouse, it was getting lighter. It was like the nighttime was being sucked away to leave daylight.

Wow! The Catskills were stranger than I had ever imagined!

"Hee, hee," Uncle Horace giggled. "I love this part!"

The vortex seemed to have a mind of its own. It grew longer, reaching out over the driveway. Sometimes it went up in the air, sometimes it sniffed along the ground. But wherever it went, it sucked up the artificial night Grimlo had called up a few hours earlier.

Then I understood. The strange clock in my uncle's front room, the one that looked like a huge sundial, only made it *look* like it was night on the farm. It was a way that Uncle Horace could enter the gargoyle realm anytime he wanted. But Grimlo had set the clock to 11:59, giving us only so many hours of artificial night. And that time was now up. The gargoyle night was disappearing, and we'd soon be back to daytime. That's why the vortex was here. To suck up the artificial gargoyle night and set the time back to normal.

"I always *bark!* this part when it *bark! bark!*" Gerty said strangely.

"Hey, what's happening to Gerty?" I asked. "Is she alright?"

"Nothing to worry about, Milo," Horace said. "That's just the gargoyle magic wearing off."

"*Bark! bark!* until it *bark!*" Gerty tried again. Then just shook her head and waited.

We watched as the night disappeared and daylight returned. The yard was back to normal, as well as the driveway. Bright sun shined down on the house and yard.

The vortex was cleaning up the dark woods, and it still had a bit of night sky to suck up around the hill. But soon it would all be gone.

I was kind of sad to see it go, and wondered when we'd get another chance to visit the gargoyle realm.

Uncle Horace walked down the steps and onto the grass. "Stay on the porch," he said to us. "That vortex is unpredictable sometimes."

"What are you doing?" I asked.

"Just making sure everything gets cleaned up proper."

That's when I saw the Spickelark.

As if in slow motion, I saw the bird swoop out of a dark space that hovered in the forest. The last remaining bit of gargoyle night. I saw it glide towards Uncle Horace. I saw his talisman, the same bit of Moonstone that hung around my neck, hanging outside his shirt. Then a terrible thought occurred to me.

"Look out!" I cried.

An instant later the Spickelark had snatched the talisman from around his neck. Uncle Horace grabbed at the bird, but it climbed just out of his reach. It fluttered and almost fell, the talisman throwing off its balance. But it righted itself and turned towards the retreating vortex. It had meant to steal it all along.

"Come back here!" he yelled, and began to chase after it.

At the same time, Gerty barked and went plowing down the steps after the bird. She passed my uncle in a flash.

The vortex swung around in the air, sucking up the last bit of darkness. It was getting smaller now that it was running out of fuel.

"NOOO!!" Grimlo yelled. "Gerty, come ba—!" But his voice cut off. I turned and saw him wobbling on the front porch, trying to speak, but his mouth shut tight. There was too little magic left in the air.

Gerty was hot on the heels of the Spickelark. She was gaining ground. The bird was about to escape. The vortex was getting smaller. Gerty was almost to the creek bed.

And just like that, Gerty jumped at the bird with the Moonstone necklace hanging from its beak. And as Gerty leaped, a Snarlok tentacle reached out of the vortex, grabbing for the Moonstone. It had been another trick! The Spickelark was helping the Snarloks! Gerty grabbed the necklace with her mouth just as the Snarlok grabbed the necklace. They crashed together in midair. And with a flash of light, the vortex closed, and Gerty was gone.

A STRANGE
HAPPENING

Standing on the front porch of my uncle's farmhouse, we all stared in disbelief. One minute we had been celebrating our successful journey into the gargoyle realm, and the next, Gerty and the talisman were gone.

"Gerty?" Uncle Horace said in disbelief. He had stopped running when she disappeared, and was now shambling forward like a man in a trance. He was slowly making his way to where the vortex had been. But there was nothing but sunshine and a light breeze.

"Gerty?" he said distantly.

"Uncle Horace!" I yelled. I started down the steps, but stopped. I turned to my friends, looking for confirmation that the whole thing had just happened.

My friends were silent. For a second I thought they had somehow lost their voices too. Either that, or I was losing my marbles.

I looked at Sammy and said, "Did you just see that?"

"See it? Of course I did! Gerty got sucked up!"

"And you?" I pointed at Suzy.

"Yes, I saw it," she said. "Poor Gerty."

"We all did," Kat said. "It actually happened. I just… I don't know what to do now."

We watched as Uncle Horace slowly made his way across the dry creek bed. He wandered aimlessly up the hill looking for Gerty.

"His talisman," Sammy said. "Now that it's gone, what happens?"

"Now that it's gone," Suzy said, "he can't get back into the gargoyle realm to help Gerty."

"Can he still perform the ritual?" Kat asked.

I wasn't sure. I wasn't sure of anything just then.

"Grimlo," I said, "what do we do now?"

Grimlo stood silent. A cement garden gnome with a stony look.

"Grimlo?" I asked again.

"What happened to Grimlo?" Kat asked.

"It's daytime," said Suzy. "He can't talk during the day, remember? Unless he's in the house. Quick, carry him inside!"

I grabbed Grimlo and we went inside. The owl clock had stopped flying and was sitting on its carved branch. The gnomon on the sundial had stopped ticking. Everything looked normal.

I sat Grimlo on the floor.

BOINGGG! He sprung up like a top.

"Ayyee, thought you'd never bring me in!" he said. "Too much pollywaggin' goin' on fer a 'mergency of this magnormous proportion!"

"What happened?" I asked. "Where's Gerty? And what do we do now?"

"Hold yer horses," Grimlo said. "I got to make sure the Sands O' Time are still runnin' right."

He sprung up and down off the couch and chairs, checking the strange hourglasses, tweaking knobs and listening to the shadow on the sundial slide across the clock face.

"Time!" Suzy said. "Oh, gosh, what time is it?" And looked at her watch. "Hey, wait a minute. How is that possible? My watch says it's only 4:47. That's only about twenty minutes AFTER the time we left. But we've been gone for hours!"

"A time machine," Sammy whispered. His eyes went wide. "Milo, your uncle invented a time machine!"

"Not a… time… machine," Grimlo said in between hops and hourglass adjustments. "More of a… time… jiggler."

"A time jiggler?" Sammy said. "What's that?"

"We didn't go back in time," said Suzy. "Uncle Horace's machine just sort of… stopped time? I guess." She shrugged her shoulders.

"But did it really stop?" Kat asked. "It didn't stop in the gargoyle realm."

"But we thought time runs differently there anyway," I said.

Finally, Grimlo landed in a chair with a loud THUMP! and leaned back. "Whew! I'm gettin' too old fer this line ah work. I think I need to get me a job on me brother's boat stowing the jib-thingies."

"You can't!" I yelled. "Holy cow! Gerty! The talisman! What are we going to do now?"

"Oh, Blackbeard!" Grimlo said. "That's right. OK, now listen up. You all did a fine job finding Horace. And yes, this here contraption of his, well… he needed a way to travel into the realm without havin' to wait for nighttime to come around. So, he invented this thing. As long as someone is here to work it, there's usually no problem gettin' back here before someone knows you're gone. You come back at the same time. We just spent another twenty minutes jawin' on the porch."

"Awesome!" said Kat. "So we can go in anytime we want?"

"And get back before our parents know we're gone?" asked Sammy.

"Pretty much," said Grimlo. "Assuming the thing don't go haywire. Or the Owl don't fly out the window and get lost. Heh, there was this one time—"

Grimlo stopped. "Errr, uh, well… no need to worry about that. Now, let's talk about what we have to do next."

He sprung over to the corner of the room by the large front window. Sitting almost unnoticed was a weird old table with some type of metal cover. I didn't remember seeing it before, but then again, there was so much stuff in this room it was overwhelming.

Grimlo pulled a small stool out from beneath the table and hopped onto it. Pushing a hidden button in the side of the table, a series of clanks and clunks emanated from the table just as a mechanical arm started moving. The metal cover was attached to the mechanical arm, and slowly rose off the table. It settled into position above the table. It was a strange mirror.

The table was covered by a piece of glass. When the metal piece rose, it began to reflect what was beneath the glass top. There was a map in the table!

We all gathered around behind Grimlo. Some of us peered over his shoulder looking down at the map beneath the glass. Some just watched the reflection of the map in the mirror. But we were all amazed to see the same map that Uncle Horace had drawn in Suzy's field guide. But there was one big difference.

"Wow!" said Sammy. "It's moving."

"What?" we all said, crowding in.

Sammy was right. It *was* moving! We just couldn't tell *what* the moving things were.

Grimlo was muttering to himself as he watched the map. "Aye… hmmm… grrr…"

"What is it?" Kat asked. "What do you see?"

"This here is a map of the realm of the gargoyles," he said. "Just like the one Suzy has, only you can see what might be happenin'."

"It looks like ants," Sammy said. "A bunch of ants moving around in sand."

"That there would be my kin and relations," Grimlo said, gruffly.

"Oh, sorry," said Sammy.

"And that there," Grimlo pointed to a dot doing crazy loops. "Would be me brother Hammerling, sailing his ship."

It looked like a drunk ant to me, but I didn't say that. I could understand why the spot on the map was doing crazy loops now.

"But where has Gerty gone off to?" Grimlo said to himself.

"Gerty?" I said. "We can see Gerty on here?"

"Should be able to," said Grimlo. "I just can't get a bead on her."

"But why should we be able to see her?" Suzy asked.

Grimlo turned around and looked at her. "Because of that." He pointed to the Moonstone necklace around Suzy's neck.

"This?"

"Aye, Gerty has one on her collar. A chip of Moonstone, I mean."

"She does?" I said. "I didn't know that."

"Aye, she does. And it's the bit of Moonstone that should be showin' up on— wait!" Grimlo pulled a pair of spectacles out from the inside of his coat. He looked at us as if he was embarrassed to put them on, then grunted and put them on anyway. He leaned close to the glass top.

"Oh, Blackbeard!" said Grimlo. "Not that way Gerty! Don't go that way!"

"Which way?" I asked. "What's happened to Gerty?"

Grimlo removed his glasses, turned and looked at us all. "Whatever's got Gerty ain't good. I can see the blip of her talisman, but just barely. They're taking her deep."

"Oh man," Sammy moaned.

"Where?" asked Kat. "Who is it, and where are they taking Gerty?"

Grimlo hopped from the bench to the sundial table. "You kids head home and rest up. Come back here the day after tomorrow, at noon. I got to get my plans made."

"What plans?" we all said together.

"Whatever's got Gerty is takin' her west. You get rested up and be here at noon, the day after tomorrow. I'll tell you the plan then."

"But shouldn't we do something now?" asked Kat. "We have the time-jiggler right there." She pointed to the sundial. "We could be right back in an instant."

Grimlo shook his head. "Nay, it ain't like that. Messin' with the Sands O' Time can't be done lightly. And there's conse-squenches to be paid when you do. You have to rest up, like I said. Day after tomorrow. Then we'll be ready."

"Where are we going?" I asked.

Grimlo looked very seriously at each one of us. "Where your uncle ain't never been. So, there's no map fer it. You're going into Westworld."

THANKS AND A SNEAK PEEK

Dear reader,

My sincere thanks for reading *The Secret of the Moonstone*, the first book in my *Milo Savage Series*. I hope you enjoyed reading it as much as I did writing it!

By way of a small thank you, here's a sneak peek at the second book in the series, *The Curse of the Chimera,* coming soon!

Enjoy!

D.S. Quinton

THE CURSE OF THE CHIMERA

G rimlo was right, gargoyle hunting was tiring work.

And to be honest, my friends and I hadn't *really* been hunting gargoyles. Not yet anyway. But we had just rescued my Uncle Horace from a rogue band of them.

But that still meant we had ventured into the gargoyle realm, avoided the booby traps, solved the riddles of the four monkey sisters, and done a bunch of other cool stuff. I hadn't had that much fun since the time I snuck the fake eyeballs into the punchbowl at the Girl Scouts cookie drive.

And yeah, I got in trouble for that, too.

But Grimlo was right, gargoyle hunting was tiring work. I was exhausted.

After my friends went home, I sat on the old couch in the front room of my uncle's farmhouse. Uncle Horace was still searching Gargoyle Hill for Gerty, his lost English Sheepdog, but I knew he wouldn't find her there. She'd just disappeared into the vortex.

I watched the Sands of Time run through the strange hourglasses that hung from the walls. Each one running at a different speed. Even backwards. I watched as the grains flowed back and forth, back and forth, and my eyelids grew heavy. I laid my head on a pillow to rest.

*

Later that night, I awoke to a faint scratching sound.

Scritch, scritch, scritch.

What was that? I thought, sleepily. I opened my blurry eyes and sat up in bed.

In bed?

I looked around my dark room sitting silently on the third floor of my uncle's farmhouse.

How did I get up here?

I briefly imagined myself sleepwalking, like a zombie, up the stairs and into my room. I remembered when I used to do the zombie-shuffle for my friends at my old school. But back then it was just for laughs. Now, here in the creepy Catskill Mountains, the strange things that were happening were more than playground jokes. There was real danger in these mountains.

Scritch, scritch, scritch.

There it was again! I got out of bed and tiptoed to the window. The wood floorboards creaking beneath my feet. I peered out through the glass. Maybe a tree branch was moving against the side of the house, I thought.

It was pitch black outside. The only light came from the strange lampposts that stood around the farm.

A shadow moved.

Yikes! What's out there?

My uncle's house sat by itself on the side of a hill. Its three-story height and steep roof towered above everything around it. I shouldn't be seeing any shadows move up here, I thought. Unless they were made by something that could fly.

Gargoyles, I thought.

Did I just see the shadow of a gargoyle fly outside my window?

But that shouldn't be possible. There was no mist on Gargoyle Hill so the entrance to the gargoyle realm was closed. The Dance of the Gargoyles was still days away. Besides, gargoyles couldn't get out of the realm and move around in the human world. Could they?

I began to wonder.

The Snarloks had found a way to reach into the human world on two occasions that I knew of. And even though it had just been with their tentacles, it had still been pretty scary. And it hadn't been my imagination.

Another shadow! Something ran across the lawn.

Or someone.

The shadow was large and mishappen, but one thing was certain; it'd had legs. Something with legs was lurking in the shadows outside the house.

I put my hands to the sides of my face, shielding out any light. I scanned over the lawn looking for the trespasser.

Scritch, scritch, scritch.

There was the sound again! Right next to my window! It sounded like something was clawing its way up the wall of my uncle's house. Maybe it was a gargoyle trying to break into my window.

But why?

I hadn't done anything to the gargoyles to make them mad.

Well...

My friends and I *had* fought several of them just recently.

And we *had* stabbed several Snarlok tentacles with arrows.

And then there was the narrow escape we'd made on Hammerling's flying boat...

So yeah, I could see how they might be kind of mad.

Scritch, scratch...

The thing was getting closer. I could almost feel it crawling up the outside wall.

Scratch...

Scratch...

I strained my eyes to left. It was really close now.

Scratch, scritch...

A little gargoyle face appeared right in front of me!

"AHH!" I yelled, jerking back from the window.

"GORP!" The thing yelled in fright.

For a brief second our eyes locked. We looked at each other through the thin pane of glass. Then it began to wobble.

I watched in slow motion as the gargoyle outside my window began to fall backwards. Its large eyes went wide with fright. Large floppy ears wiggled nervously. Its short arms waved in the air, trying to catch its balance. Stone wings flapped uselessly trying to fly.

"Gorp?" it said in a confused, scared voice.

Then it fell backwards into the dark.

I jumped back to the window, pressing my face to the glass, but it was already out of sight. I listened for the sound of something hitting the ground. Everything was quiet.

I listened for the scratching sound the little thing had made when it had climbed the wall to my window. Nothing.

The gargoyle was gone.

I sat on my bed, staring out the window in confusion. *How was this possible? What did this mean?*

Shadows running around my house? Gargoyle faces outside my window?

I didn't understand how this had happened, but I was sure of one thing.

Gargoyles were on the loose.

—

Curse of the Chimera will be available in 2023 from Amazon.

Keep up to date at dsquinton.com!

ACKNOWLEDGEMENTS

Thanks again to my wonderful wife Mary. This book is far better because of your steadfast support.

ABOUT THE AUTHOR

D.S. Quinton was born in the Midwest USA and grew up playing baseball, swimming and daydreaming about magical creatures. Sort of like Milo.

He read a lot, including Greek mythology. Some of his favorite stories can be found in:

The Earthsea Trilogy by Ursula K. Leguin
The Chronicles of Narnia by C.S. Lewis
The Dragonlance Series by Laura and Tracy Hickman

He will continue writing about Milo and his friends, so stay tuned. Now that the gargoyle realm has been discovered, there will be a lot to explore. And don't forget about the creepy gargoyle music. It was hard for him to get it recorded without getting squooshed.

OTHER BOOKS BY D.S. QUINTON

D.S. Quinton also has a series of adult novels, novellas and short stories. Look for these titles:

The Spirit Hunter Series (Supernatural Horror Thriller)
The Circus Sideshow Series (Supernatural Oddity)
The Evolution Series (Technothriller)

And some miscellaneous short stories